Dreams of
STARS AND LIES

Dreams of
STARS AND LIES

JEAN DAVIS

All characters, places and events portrayed in this novel are fictional. No resemblance to any specific person, place or event is intended.

Dreams of Stars and Lies

www.jeandavisauthor.com

ISBN-13:   (print) 978-1-7345701-4-4
                 (ebook) 978-1-7345701-5-1

First Edition: June 2020

Published by StreamlineDesign LLC

Also by Jean Davis

The Last God
Sahmara
A Broken Race
Destiny Pills and Space Wizards

The Narvan
Trust
Chain of Gray

TABLE OF CONTENTS

ACKNOWLEDGEMENTS

These stories wouldn't be what they are today without the inspiration and assistance of others. Thanks to Poet Michael D. Jones, Melissa Haveman of Creatively Centered, Stella Telleria, and Joan H. Young.

BATTERY

Glass walls surrounded Celia's narrow bed and the small table with two chairs. A pristine quiet square amidst the chaos of the warehouse. The white coats were busy today, sipping their coffee while buzzing around between desks and equipment. As always, two pairs of eyes watched her.

Sitting atop the fluffy white comforter, her legs crossed and her pillow clutched to her chest, Celia watched them back. Over the years she'd watched Raymond's hair turn grey and wrinkles creep further out from Charlotte's eyes. Today, the pink of her lipstick had already feathered into the lines around her lips. When Celia had first arrived here, Charlotte had held her hand, leading her into what Charlotte called the 'special playroom'. The woman had seemed so tall, towering over Celia as she'd led the way into the room Celia still sat in so many years later.

The toys were gone through. They hadn't been pleased with how she played with them.

No one held her hand anymore either. In fact, no one touched her at all. Everything was passed through a two-part slot in the door.

Raymond and Charlotte spent the morning in their chairs, talking without looking at one another, keeping their eyes on her. Celia watched the other white coats pointing at screens and passing papers back and forth. They all stayed back, too far for her to hear them. She passed the hours making up a conversation for them, their imagined voices playing out in her head.

Doctor Hershel came in the afternoon. His arrival allowed Raymond and Charlotte to take their lunch hour break. The Doctor's bent form shuffled closer as he dragged one of their chairs over to the speaker near the sealed slot on her door. He pressed the button that activated the speaker. A faint hum filled her room.

"Good afternoon, Celia," he said, as he always did. He settled into the chair, balancing a notepad and pen on his lap.

He didn't wait for her reply. She rarely spoke.

"I've brought something for you. Are you

hungry?"

It had been a long time since she'd eaten. Enticed by the offer, she let go of the pillow and swung her legs over the edge of the bed. Celia stood. Loose pants settled over her legs, sliding down to her feet. Celia hovered just above the floor.

"Come on then," he said.

Doctor Hershel opened the slot and slid a grey rectangle through. It landed on the shelf inside the door with a heavy thunk. Two silver nodes protruded from the top. Her hands tingled in anticipation.

Celia willed her body forward, gliding just above the floor she only guessed was smooth. She'd never touched it.

"It's fully charged," he said.

She picked up the battery and tried to ignore the horde of white coats she knew were raptly watching from behind the safety of the yellow line that surrounded her room.

If she weren't half-starved, she would have set the meal on the table and made them wait. Her favorite game was to try to catch them being unobservant. That's why they had white coats in the chairs now, to make sure someone was always watching. She sighed. The only defense she had left was to turn her back to them. Even then, she knew they had sensors and cameras all around her room. They'd still see everything, but somehow, it felt like a little victory that they couldn't see it with their own eyes.

Celia placed her hands over the cool metal of the nodes. Opening her power well, she drew from the battery. The tingle of incoming power invigorated her, but it wasn't enough. She needed more. So much more.

She dropped the empty battery back onto the shelf. A scratching sound filtered through the speaker.

"Still hungry?" The doctor put his pen down. "If you speak to me, I will get you another one."

The last time she'd spoken, the white coats had been horrified by the toys spinning through the air. It had been a wondrous day, the power inside her coalescing into something she finally understood. Something from the dim memories of her home. A place far from here.

If she could only speak to one of her own kind, she would surely understand her powers better, but the doctor and his team seemed to think she should know them all on her own.

"You can do so much, Celia. Those who found you told us of great miracles done by your people. Don't you want to do glorious things? There is far more to life than sitting on that bed all day."

There was nothing more for her. The white

coats made sure of that.

"We've been at an impasse for far too long, my dear. If we don't start making progress, our little endeavor here will be terminated. His cloudy blue eyes drilled into her from the other side of the glass. "Do you understand what I mean?"

Celia blinked once, engaging her secondary vision. Inside the doctor, his system moved sluggishly, the large muscle in his chest pumping at an inadequate rate. Doctor Hershel wouldn't be coming to see her much longer. Not that she would tell him so.

His age-spotted hand curled into a fist atop his writing-filled page. "I know you understand me, Celia. You understand everything here. You're a smart girl. We have the scans to prove it. Years of data."

The doctor's fist thumped hard on the glass. "What I need are results. And if you want to keep breathing, you're going to provide them. Is that clear enough for you?"

Celia looked beyond the doctor to the milling white coats, all of them watching but doing their best to not appear to be doing so. Undoubtedly, they heard every word that passed through her speaker.

She licked her lips and peered into the closest camera. The perpetually patient doctor had never spoken to her with force before. If his team was truly desperate for results, she might be able to get another meal out of him. And that might just be enough.

Picking up the dead battery, she held it up to the glass in front of his face.

"Interested?"

She nodded.

"Give me a moment." He stood and set the pad and pen in the chair.

As he started to walk away, she tapped the glass. If he wanted results, she needed something to work with.

Startled, he turned back to her.

Celia scanned the desks beyond the bright light shining down from the high ceiling. A vase of yellow flowers caught her attention. She pointed to it.

He nodded. Within minutes he was back in his chair with another battery and a handful of flowers, their wet stems dripping on the floor.

"Results first."

He dropped the flowers through the slot. A lovely fragrance tickled her nose. Celia gathered up the tangle of stems and brought the flowers to her face, breathing deep.

"You're going to have to do more than enjoy Sheila's flowers." The doctor tapped his pen on his knee.

Setting the bouquet on the table, she picked up a single yellow petal that had fallen on the floor. A drop of water slipped from its silken surface. The clear orb stuck to her finger. Turning her hand over, she played with the droplet of water until the language of it became clear in her mind. The sounds of the petal took longer but they also began to whisper, taunting her with hints of the living thing it had fully been.

She breathed deep, inhaling the scent of the bouquet on the table beside her and the moisture of the water sprinkled across the glossy white surface. Rubbing the soft petal between her fingers, she examined the words in her head more closely.

On the other side of the glass, where undoubtedly the entire team of white coats was glued to a sensor or camera feed, she noted little movement. Here inside her room, for once, everything was alive, the very air full of words in the language of the flower and the water. She tested the sounds of it all on her tongue, still keeping her voice to herself. Within the purity of those words, others lurked, broken and disjointed. She puzzled through the missing sections, filling in gaps as her understanding increased.

Other tiny fragments became clear as she sorted through the words: Soil, small grains protesting their removal from the greater whole, along with cast-off skin cells of Doctor Hershel and others that must belong to Sheila.

While the flower, the soil, and the water shared their stories with her, it was the skin that intrigued her most. Its language unfurled slowly, a complex tangle of microscopic proportions. Celia let her mind work on that problem while she allowed the first words in nine years to dance along her tongue. She opened her mouth and let them fly free.

The soil multiplied, flowing across the surface of the table. Rich brown particles swelled, layers upon layers, until they were several fingers deep. Through it all, green shoots burst forth. They surged upward, sprouting leaves and stems.

There she paused in her litany to gaze at the doctor. His mouth hung open. He stood now, his face pressed to the glass. The pen and paper lay on the floor by his feet. Not a sound other than the faint hiss came through the speaker.

"You wish to see more?" she asked in the weak and empty language he spoke.

His gaze lifted from the table garden to her face as if fully seeing her for the first time. He nodded.

She pointed to the battery.

"Oh yes, of course." He opened the slot and

dropped it through.

The second charge flowed through her faster than the first, doubling the fuel in the well they'd always kept so close to empty. The words in her mind pulsed and clarified, writing themselves on the very air around her. She danced over and through them, spinning in circles, arms outstretched, laughing.

She could see them now, the voices of those of her kind who had come long before, who had spoken into creation these very people and everything they surrounded themselves with. She wasn't alone. The whispers of her distant family were all around her.

Buds swelled at the tops of the stems in the spontaneous garden atop the table. Yellow flowers erupted, filling the room with their sweet scent. The smell, a shout of joy all of its own.

Through all of the delight surrounding her, it was the sound of the male and female skin she listened to the closest. Within that skin, the inner workings of the body just outside the glass started to become clear. The dysfunctional muscle at Doctor Hershel's center held her interest for a moment as she considered which words might correct it.

Then she spotted the electric pulses running through his body. Celia eyed the empty battery on the shelf inside the door.

With the extra power flowing in her well, she could finally catch the faint language of the glass. The hard and hollow words bucked and twisted until she tamed them with her tongue, her own words flowing back out into the glorious symphony that filled the room.

With a loud crash, the walls shattered, spilling into a mountain of jagged shards on the polished concrete outside the room.

Someone screamed. Celia's second sight flickered back into focus, revealing the mass of power waiting for her on the other side of the yellow line. But first, she reached out to the doctor. His skin was warm and soft.

He gasped as she placed her hands on either side of his face.

Celia spoke the language of man, unraveling the ties that bound the sparks of power contained within their flesh.

Throughout the room bodies melted to the floor while energy flowed toward her and into her well. The white coats lay silent. Empty.

For the first time in her life, her well was full. Celia basked in the feeling of completeness. Her skin glowed, burning away the clothes the white coats had given her and covering her instead in a brilliant light.

The words of the soil came easily to her now. She filled the floor with a thick covering of the rich loam she had started on the tabletop. Green shoots popped from its surface.

Celia settled her feet into the fluffy cool soil, feeling it squish between her toes. This was so much better than the dead surface on which her room had been built.

By the time Celia reached the door, her well was overflowing. She walked outside. Sunlight filled the blue sky high above, but chaos reigned all around her. So many dead surfaces towering, blocking out the horizon in all directions. Metal monsters sped through the sky and along the ground. The air itself was ill and through all the noise trapped in each and every molecule, it cried out for salvation.

Closing her eyes, she listened for the words. There were so many. So much to learn, so much left behind by those who had come long before her. Had they known what would become of what they created or had they grown tired of the mess those creations had made and moved along?

Longing to see what a perfect world could be, an example to go by for her future, Celia began to speak. She pulled soil up through the hard surfaces and shook the towers apart by untangling the elements that had built them, bringing everything within reach back to its natural state. It didn't take long for her well to gutter and her strength to wane.

She looked into the pocket of peaceful quiet she'd created and called forward the people gawking at what she'd done. The truth of it was plain then, with so many gathered closely. Ancient language swirled them.

A host of people surged toward her, crying out, begging, pleading. Their words fell empty and powerless amidst the beauty surrounding her.

It would take time to repair all the damage that had been done, but she had a renewable energy source. Celia's attention darted through the exodus of fleeing people, selecting healthy young ones and drawing them to her.

They had taken her from her kind, but with the energy they provided, Celia would travel to as many worlds as it took. She would follow the trail of batteries her family had left behind and the clues in the language they spoke, filling the universe with glorious miracles until she found them once again.

DEVOLUTION

Marion choked back a sob and reached for the box of tissues on the corner of the doctor's desk. Paul sat by her side, nodding at the doctor as if everything was fine.

"Mrs. Karrington, the results shouldn't be a surprise. With your family history of illness and early death, surely you didn't expect to be allowed to bear children?"

Marion looked to her husband for support, but his face was turned to the wall hung with black-framed certificates which boasted degrees in reproductive evaluations, research, and sciences. Accreditations from various organizations and government agencies flanked the degrees like a crowd condemning Marion for her genetic downfalls.

She wiped the tears from her cheeks. "My father was eighty-six. That isn't young."

"If we lived a hundred years ago, I might be more inclined to agree with you." The doctor flipped his screen around, confronting her with her own medical records. "However, our focus is on reducing healthcare costs and overpopulation. You do read the news, don't you, Mrs. Karrington?"

Paul finally looked at her, but it wasn't out of concern. His tight-lipped scowl informed her that she was embarrassing him.

Marion squeezed the tissue into a tiny pellet with her shaking hand. "Of course. It's just that I'd hoped that with Paul's strong genes, mine would bear less weight when it came to attaining our approval."

"I'm sorry, Mrs. Karrington. We take both parental lines into account."

The windowed wall behind the doctor provided a view of the traffic flying against the grey-blue sky. They didn't even rate a single window in their apartment, yet the doctor got an entire wall, like he was some kind of god.

Marion returned her gaze to the man who held the fate of her unconceived child in his hands. "I promise we will stop at one. Please." She felt her control slipping away and took a deep, shuddering breath in the hopes of regaining a little of it. "Paul's brothers and sisters have been allowed six children each. Each! I'm only asking for one."

The doctor frowned. He turned the screen back around and closed his tablet. "If every substandard candidate was granted one child, we'd be no better off than we were before. That is what history is there for, Mrs. Karrington, for us to learn from."

Marion closed her eyes and let the last sliver of control go. Once the doctor filed his judgment there wouldn't be a second chance. Her dreams of motherhood would go the way of her dreams of a happy marriage. Paul had killed those weeks after their wedding when he'd given up being the considerate, charismatic man she'd fallen in love with. "Please. I don't have any family left. I am the last of my line. Is one more generation too much to ask for?"

"Yes. This is the way the world works, Mrs. Karrington. The weak fall away so the strong can survive."

Paul glared at her.

"You can't know that our offspring would carry my genetic weaknesses. I have talents and gifts. I have something to offer." Her voice rose. "I've worked my assigned job for twenty-four years with good reviews. I've paid the government its due without complaint. I've fulfilled my community service hours each year with a smile. I've done everything asked of me. Why can't you allow me this one little thing?"

The doctor tapped a button on the wide wristband just below the stiff white cuff of his shirt. "Send security to my office immediately."

"There's no need for that." Paul stood and waved Marion to her feet.

"Sir, I should warn you that your wife's family records indicate a propensity for mental instability. Are you sure you wouldn't like some assistance?"

Marion shot to her feet. "I'm right here. Don't talk about me like I'm not."

Paul's scowl deepened. He shook his head. "I am accustomed to dealing with my wife."

"I will note your refusal of assistance." The doctor tapped his wristband again and then opened his tablet to type a few words. "You will be held responsible for her appearance at her sterilization appointment next week. Should she fail to appear, you will both find your citizen rights and privileges reduced."

Paul grabbed her arm, digging his fingers into her flesh as he steered her toward the door. "She will be there. Thank you for your time."

The door closed. Pain erupted in her arm as Paul tightened his grip. "Are you trying to get us both arrested?" He hauled her to the lift.

"No, of course not." Marion bowed her head and followed along numbly to the roof where they took a public transport to their plex. The lift from the rooftop landing zone on their plex seemed to take hours to reach their mid-level floor.

"Snap out of it. I humored you with the appointment like you asked. Sterilization isn't the end of the world." Paul opened the door to their apartment and pushed her inside.

Marion backed away from him. "It's the end of mine. Do you ever stop thinking about yourself?"

His mouth hung open for a split second and then snapped shut. "Are you really that delusional that you thought we would be cleared to have children? I never wanted any. That's why I married you. You got my mother off my back about settling down, and I snubbed her by not giving her any more grandchildren. She has enough of those already." He shook his head. "Borrow one of my nieces or nephews. That will cure you of your desire soon enough."

"I don't want nieces and nephews." And, she wanted to say, 'I don't want to be married to you'. She cursed the government who decreed divorce illegal and herself for falling for Paul's charming act. Tears burned in her eyes. "I want a child of our own."

A child of *her* own would have been better, but she needed Paul or the labs would laugh in her face.

"What's the difference? Is it the bigger housing allotment? I'll see if I can pull a few strings."

"No." She didn't mind their seven hundred square feet of space. It was almost double the size of the apartment where she'd grown up. "Don't you want to hear a child laugh, to hold your hand, to ask you to read stories and play?"

"Get a hold of reality, Marion. I don't want my privileges reduced to pay for your psychiatric care." He ran a hand over his face. "We haven't seen Michael's kids in a couple of weeks. Give their nanny a call."

"Blessed with six children and they don't care about any of them. What is this world coming to?" She wiped the tears from her cheeks. "Don't you see? I would care about our child. No nannies, no month-long pleasure trips away from them. I want to watch them grow up; help them learn to walk, to speak, to read. I want a child of my own that looks like me."

Paul sighed. "And here I thought you had one reasonable thought in your head when you told the doctor you hoped our child would take after me rather than you." He sat in one of the two chairs by the table in the kitchen. "Tell me you had the presence of mind to order our dinner. I'm hungry."

She forced her voice to a semblance of steady. "I placed the order before breakfast like I do every morning."

He crossed his arms over his chest.

She went to the white cabinet on the wall that hung over the narrow counter and opened the door. Two plates sat inside with steak, potatoes, green beans and a grain-studded roll on each. She removed the plates and set them on the table along with two glasses of water.

"Steak again?" Paul shook his head. "What was the other choice?"

"Lasagna." She took a bite of the tasteless but tender, synthetic meat.

"That would have been better. We had steak twice already this week."

"Sorry."

Marion finished her meal in silence and moved to the couch where she sat staring blindly at the evening news. A reporter's voice droned on about plex overcrowding in a distant city. People were rioting and the military was being called in to assist with security.

"Change that. You don't need to be watching that sort of savage behavior. We give people simple and orderly processes for requesting expansion and still they resort to this." He shook his head. "They should just let the military wipe the plex clean so more civilized people can move in."

She spun around. "You're talking about killing women and children, entire families. How can you say such a thing?"

"You've got your head so wrapped up in this baby nonsense, you've forgotten how to see reason. I'm going to get some work done before bed." He slipped into the tiny room he used as an office and closed the door.

She flipped through her viewing options and came across a documentary of the wilds. Sweeping footage brought crumbling stone walls and toppled towers of glass and steel into the room. Tall grasses swayed in winds that blew through crumbled asphalt fields. Humanity's sprawling swaths of wreckage floated before her in a panoramic display. Creatures with teeth and claws slunk between decaying structures, prowling for a meal. The narrator spewed facts about the first plexes, those chosen to live there, and how within fifty years, everyone had come together to make the world a better, cleaner, and more peaceful place. Prisoners had once been cast out, sentenced to meet their fate in the wilds, but the government had put a stop to that, calling it inhumane punishment.

The narrator portrayed the advent of plex

living as a new age for mankind: Everyone working in coordination for a brighter future. Though she'd read her required history lessons as a child, she still couldn't imagine life out there, outside a plex, in the dirt, with bugs and wild beasts, not knowing where your next meal would come from. She turned off the program before it gave her nightmares and went to bed.

The light in Paul's office clicked off, and a few minutes later, his larger form sank into the mattress beside her. The movement filled the blankets with a gust of cold air. She shivered and pulled them tighter around herself.

"I trust you will go to your sterilization appointment without any more of this crazy talk?" His voice grew harder. "It's your own fault for wanting to see the doctor, you know. Had you accepted the way things are without throwing a tantrum about having children, you wouldn't have to go through sterilization. Now we're stuck paying for that as well as the doctor visit."

"I'm sorry." Marion hated how meek she sounded.

He grumbled something under his breath and rolled over.

She was tired of being meek. Even when she followed the rules and acted the way people wanted her to, she never got what she wanted. "I could stop taking the birth control."

He sat up and turned the bedside light on. His eyes were wide as he stared at her. "Stop eating? You'd starve in the time it took for the drugs to fade from your system."

"We could share your meal."

"If you think I'm going hungry just so you can cheat the system, you're very wrong."

Her heart pounded faster. She sat up beside him. "But we could do it. We'd get by. And we don't have to use the lab. We could go about this naturally."

"Assuming we don't starve, you mean. Yes, you could grossly distort your body, endure nine months of tremendous discomfort and go naked the majority of the time, because none of the clothes we have would fit you. And don't forget that you wouldn't be able to leave the apartment, because once you're showing, you'd be turned in. You'd lose your job, which would also raise suspicion and cut further into our finances." The muscles along his jaw twitched, and the veins in his neck stood out. "No one would help you deliver the baby, you insane woman!"

"People had babies on their own all the time before labs became popular."

"And women died. Babies died. Do you want to die, Marion? I'd rather you didn't." His voice shook. "Do you want your precious baby to die?

The labs keep babies safe and ensure healthy children. I'm taking you to a psychiatrist in the morning. The doctor was right. You need help."

Talking with a psychiatrist wouldn't help prevent her sterilization. The doctor had made it quite clear that government employees could not be swayed by impassioned speeches or tears.

"Go to sleep. We're leaving right after breakfast. I don't want to hear another word." Paul turned the light out, settled back under the blankets, and rolled over.

She stared at the ceiling until her eyes closed. The joyful faces of mothers carrying their infants filled her head. She wanted so badly to be one of those women that she could smell the sweet baby scent. Their cooing made her warm inside, their tiny fingers wrapping around a single one of her own. She shopped for the perfect outfits, decorated the room, assembled the crib and picked out names. Paul held their son, and for the first time since they'd been married, he truly smiled at her. Her heart swelled. A lump formed in her throat. This was the man she'd loved, the one that had made her feel special, that had picked her out of the crowd and lifted her up to his station. This was the life they were meant to share.

"Wake up already." Paul nudged her in the side with his elbow. "I've made an appointment for you. We're leaving in forty minutes."

The ride in the transport was silent but for the chatter of others. She wondered what the psychiatrist was going to say that the doctor and Paul hadn't. He seemed so convinced that this was the thing that would shake sense into her. That fact alone made her palms sweat.

They exited the transport at the same dock they had the day before and made their way down to the medical zone. A receptionist showed them into an office twice as large as their bedroom. It was tidy and contained minimal furniture, three chairs, two low tables, and a lamp. A plant sat under a grow light in the corner, a single reminder of the world outside deep within the center of the plex. Its leaves were brown at the edges, but the pot was spotless.

A woman in a dark brown suit came in. She nodded to Paul. "Thank you for bringing her in. If you could wait in the lobby, please?"

Paul left without protest. Marion's stomach twisted into knots. He knew what was going to happen. This woman was on his side, not hers.

"Hello, I'm Doctor Barnes." She sat, straight-backed with perfect posture and daintily crossed her legs at the ankles. "Now then, Mrs. Karrington, can you tell me why you're here?"

"I want a child."

"I see." She picked up a tablet from the table

beside her and clinked her manicured nails over its surface.

"And why do you think you require a child to be happy?"

"I don't *require* one. I just thought it would be nice. Isn't it something most women want?"

The doctor's red lips went tight. "Not really, no. Children are a big responsibility. They require work and devotion. They're a distraction from your husband and your duty to society. They are necessary for the continuation of our kind, but not something we must all contribute. There is a process for this and it's there for a reason. Can you tell me, Marion...can I call you Marion?"

Marion nodded, knowing she'd already lost. Even trying to relate to another woman wasn't working in her favor. No one wanted to hear her side.

"Why do you feel entitled to create a child?"

"I don't feel entitled. I want to follow the rules. I just don't think the rules are fair."

"Not fair to you specifically. I see." Her fingers tapped on the tablet again. "And why is that?"

Marion tried to sit as straight as the doctor, to feel as in control, but her spine had turned to mush and could not prevent her from slouching into the chair. She stared at the tiled floor.

"Because the rules don't allow me to have what I want."

"Exactly."

She didn't have to look at the doctor, she heard the smile in her voice.

"I'm so happy that you understand, but I want you to see why these rules are in place. These rules are not meant to be cruel, Marion. They are meant to provide the best people for our future as a whole. Let me show you." Doctor Barnes rose gracefully from her chair and crossed the room to flip a switch on the wall.

"This is a simulation based on your genetics combined with those of your husband. For a few moments, I will give you the child you so desperately desire."

The hope of a having a child, even briefly, might have filled her with delight, but the doctor's demeanor made her sweat even more. Perspiration leeched into her shirt under her arms, rolling down her ribcage in tiny droplets of embarrassment.

The doctor dimmed the lights and returned to her seat. A full-dimensional projector dropped from a portal in the ceiling. The projection field lit up, filling the room with a soft glow. In the middle of the room, just above the floor, a particle no bigger than her smallest fingernail appeared. It twisted and grew, sprouting legs and arms and a bulbous head with two tiny black specks for eyes.

The embryo grew tiny fingers and toes. Ribs appeared under its pale skin. As it grew bigger, the arms and legs moved, and facial features formed. Tiny hairs sprouted on its head. It kicked one leg to reveal it was a boy.

She had a son. Marion forgot her dread and held her breath, clenching her hands together on her lap.

The baby grew until she ached to reach out and hold him. He looked so perfect. She glanced at Doctor Barnes, waiting for the horror of her genetics to reveal itself. The doctor was busy with her tablet, ignoring the wondrous display playing before them.

The child scooted around on his stomach to face her, his wide blue eyes regarding her with curiosity. He sucked on his fingers and then a toe, displaying amazing flexibility. His hair, blonde, like hers, grew longer. He sat up and held his arms out to her.

Was she supposed to get up? Could she hold him? Would she feel his skin against hers or would he dissipate? Maybe this was the torture the doctor had in mind, seeing how long she could sit and watch her son grow before she effectively killed him by disrupting the projection. Marion stayed in her chair and took in every amazing second with her son.

He stood, growing taller with each moment. His round cheeks and pudgy arms and thighs thinned. He grinned, revealing straight teeth and the dimple she'd seen on Paul's chin when he used to laugh. Her heart swelled. Soon he stood as tall as his father with his firm jaw and her own blue eyes. His limbs were straight and strong. He reminded her of the young man she'd fallen in love with, but she loved this one for very different reasons. This was her son. And he was perfect.

The projection froze. The lights came on, making the projection less vibrant and translucent, shattering the illusion.

"He's seventeen. This is when he would die," said the doctor. "You cannot see the weakness on the outside."

The doctor stood, walking into the projection field. She waved her hand in a slicing pattern. The exterior image of her son vanished. Vessels, bone and rushing blood replaced the much more pleasing view.

"This is his heart." She pointed to a pulsing organ. "This malformation comes from your line. The valve here is weak. It will stop working properly. He will not be able to work or perform physical duties."

"Surely that's something a surgeon can fix."

Doctor Barnes cocked her head, regarding Marion with a look similar to what the baby had. "Why should they? Is he entitled to be born even though he is clearly defective? We have thousands of other children who will be born without a need for medical intervention. We don't need him."

"But..."

The doctor shook her head. "He will not even live to a maximum production age. He will not become a vital member of society. He will only be a distraction to you and your husband, a liability. There is no return on investment." She returned the projection to the exterior view and went back to her seat to make a note on her tablet.

Marion wanted to stand, to march out of the office, but her knees were too weak and the projection held her transfixed. This was her son, standing right before her, and now that she'd seen him, she wasn't about to give him up. She closed her eyes and took a deep breath, forcing her pulse to slow and her body to stop its quaking.

"Yes, I understand," she said calmly. "That makes sense. I wish the doctor we saw yesterday had explained it as well as you have. It would have saved your time and ours."

"I'm happy to hear that." The doctor

switched the projection off.

Marion gazed past the spot where her son had stood seconds ago. "I was just being selfish, I suppose."

"We all have our moments." She consulted her tablet. "I would like to see you again tomorrow morning."

"Yes, of course."

Doctor Barnes saw her to the door with her tablet in hand. Marion stopped at the desk to make her appointment. When she was finished, she found Paul and the doctor chatting in the lobby.

Paul offered her his usual lackluster smile. It so paled in comparison to the one she'd imagined earlier that her heart ached and a lump formed in her throat.

"I'm so happy you've come to your senses." He held out his arm and she took it. "I've got to get to work and so do you."

He gave her a peck on the cheek before heading off to a waiting transport. As much as she enjoyed his improved spirits, they weren't enough to sway her resolve.

She would see her son again.

Marion worked her volunteer shift in the gardens with a joyful heart. It wasn't because of the dirt on her hands or the sunlight overhead or even the spectacular view out of the top of the plex, but from the cherry tomatoes and green beans she'd hidden in her smock. When she finished her job, she folded the smock carefully and took the lift to her floor.

With half of her food swapped with Paul's and her beans and tomatoes replaced with the smuggled, untainted versions, she put dinner on the table just as Paul walked in the door.

"Hungry?" he asked.

"We worked hard in the gardens today, and I wanted to get some reading in before bed."

"It's good to see you devoting yourself to more productive things." He sat and started in on his dinner.

"Do you think they'll cancel the sterilization?" she asked.

"I hope so. It's a month's wages."

"I'm sorry I was acting so crazy."

"As long as you're better now." He ate the rest of his meal and excused himself to go work in his office.

Marion waited until she was sure he was settled in and then accessed her own tablet. She looked up old newsfeeds covering the population of the plexes. Those led her to protests and rebellions against the plex government. Not everyone had come peacefully, and as she discovered upon further digging, there had been some who hadn't come at all. Even more current, there were reports of suicides, those who chose to leave the plex and face the chaos outside. Those were few and heavily scorned in the reports. She'd never paid attention to them before now, considering those people the crazy ones. Society was better off without them.

Morning brought her second appointment. Doctor Barnes only consulted her tablet twice during their meeting and one of those was to cancel the sterilization appointment.

"I see no need to punish you financially," she said. "However, if I do see you here again with those notions, I will be required to reinstate the order."

"Yes, I understand. Thank you."

Doctor Barnes sent her on her way. She went back up to the gardens to continue filling her obligatory service hours. She had two months to go before she'd receive her next long-term work assignment. Not being skilled like Paul, she was given whatever duty needed filling, usually something menial like moving supplies or furniture, cleaning empty apartments for new occupants, or inventorying supplies. Whatever it would be, she didn't have a lot of time to repair her relationship with Paul before she would be shunted out of the gardens and its wealth of untainted food.

Marion spent the next week doing exactly

as Paul asked, making sure to go to bed when he did and positioning herself next to him each night. They hadn't shared physical relations for over half a year. She hoped their renewed closeness and his better mood might lend itself to fulfilling her desires.

He didn't catch on the first week, but the halfway through the second week he did. Despite his tone and the way he had treated her, her body had missed his touch. She enjoyed their sweaty moments as much as his grunts and moans indicated that he did. The sex certainly wasn't as passionate as it had been when they'd first married, but at least it was fulfilling.

She spent her evenings reading about life outside the plexes and how it differed from the life she'd always known. Nights were spent in Paul's arms, days in the gardens, sneaking fresh food for each day's menu options. It wasn't until the end of the second month that she feared her food swapping was doing more harm than good. She couldn't keep anything down.

"Is something wrong?" Paul asked, nodding to her half-eaten dinner.

"I'm not feeling well."

"How odd."

"It is. I hope I haven't been exposed to anything in the garden."

Paul snorted. "The garden is the most

sanitary place we have. No one has been sick in our plex for years. Don't tell me you're going to make us known for that too. I'm just finally getting out from under your last episode. People talk, you know. This sort of thing leaves a black mark on both of us."

"I can't be ill. We'd know if there was an outbreak."

"Good. Then don't fake it either. It's not the kind of attention we need."

"I am aware of that." Her fingers curled into fists in her lap. Her anger soared to a level she'd not known she possessed. The tirade in her head spilled from her lips. "I'm not stupid. Just because my family doesn't rank as high as yours doesn't mean I don't know things. Not being granted the right to create a child doesn't make me mentally deficient." She shot to her feet. "You have no right to talk to me that way."

Marion left him there, gaping, and stormed off to the bedroom. She sat on the edge of the bed, clutching the bedcover and rocking back and forth. Where had that outburst come from? Tears welled in her eyes. All the hard work she'd done to repair their relationship was ruined. He wouldn't want to sleep with her now.

Hours crept by. Paul didn't come to bed.

When she finally brought herself to leave the bedroom in the morning, she found a blanket on the couch. Paul was gone. A divorce might not be in her future, but separations were not unheard of. How long until he kicked her out? Where would she go? Bile rose in her throat. She ran to the toilet and threw up.

A long shower served to put her more to rights. She got dressed and consulted her tablet. If she was sick, she didn't want to spread anything. Paul was right, being patient zero was a stigma neither of them wanted or could afford.

A quick search eliminated most known illnesses and left one clear culprit. She'd done what she'd set out to do. The first stages of the simulation she'd seen in Doctor Barnes's office were playing out inside her.

Near floating and grinning widely, she gathered up her smock and made her way to the lift. Like every other day, the garden waited for her. Only two days left until her reassignment. She gathered as much food in her smock as she dared.

Paul arrived home at his usual time but didn't say a word to her. He grabbed his plate and a glass of water and went straight to his office. He stayed there long into the night.

Marion sat in bed, wanting to tell him what they'd created, but knowing he'd haul her off to be sterilized in a heartbeat if she did. Children were created in labs, not bodies. This archaic thing she'd set out to do was ludicrous. He'd all but said so. She couldn't work if she was given a hard labor job. Regardless, she'd be showing within a month or two. People would know. They'd point and talk, and Paul would be beyond angry.

There was only one thing she could do and she'd known that from the moment she's set out on this path. Still, it wasn't an easy step to take. Her hands shook as she took several of Paul's shirts and pants from his closet. She packed all of her own things as well, folding them into the thick cloth bag she'd used to move into this apartment after their marriage. Sweating and nauseous, she waited until she couldn't hear him moving anymore. She tiptoed her way into the kitchen and tucked the smock full of stolen food into the bag. Her tablet went last.

Paul stirred on the couch. "What are you doing?" he asked, sitting up.

Marion went still, the bag hanging at her side. Why couldn't he have stayed asleep for a few more minutes? There was no lie she could tell. "Leaving."

"Just where do you plan on going?"

"That's no concern of yours."

"How can you say that?"

She took a deep breath and reached for the door.

"Marion, wait." She heard him shoving the blanket aside. "Where are you going?"

She walked out of the apartment and hurried toward the lift.

The lift doors had just about shut when she saw him emerge from the apartment, smoothing his shirt and running a hand through his hair. Their gazes met for an instant and then the door closed.

She punched the ground floor button.

"Access denied," said a recorded voice.

"Oh come on." She bit her lip and pushed the first floor button.

"Access denied."

The second floor button did not work either. The third did. Marion swore. If others got out, there had to be a way from there. Or maybe, said a little voice in her head, that's why access is now denied to the bottom-most floors. Maybe she would never leave. Maybe they'd be waiting for her on the third floor. They'd knock her out and she'd come to, childless and strapped to a bed for the rest of her days.

The lift stopped. She swallowed hard and got ready to swing her bag if she needed to fend anyone off. The lift lobby was empty.

The walls here were dirty and the floor worn. No sound came from the surrounding halls. She crept past the first few rooms, only to discover the apartment doors open. Did no one want to live this close to the bottom? With all the talk of plex overcrowding, she wondered why this whole floor, and presumably the two below were left vacant and in disrepair. It wasn't as if there weren't enough people to clean and rejuvenate them. Were people really that desperate to be far from the ground that they'd cram into the upper levels for the sake of social appearance or were the reports false, some government agenda to make them all grateful for the peaceful life and amenities of their own plex? Mindful of the fact that Paul could be sending someone after her, she didn't stand around to ponder.

Bag slapping against her back, Marion ran. She dashed down the hall, following the floor plan identical on each level above until she reached the emergency stairwell at the center of the plex. No one stood guard at the door. It wasn't even locked. She started downward, grimacing as her footsteps echoed off the metal stairs and walls. The hollow pounding followed her until she reached a spiral. She paused there only a minute to catch her breath and then plunged onward to the lighted exit sign far below.

The tall trunk of the plex went on seemingly forever. The bag grew heavy on her shoulder. Her stomach hurt and so did her feet. Then the door stood before her. She pushed it open.

The air smelled similar to the garden high above but less moist. Wind ruffled her hair. She stepped out from the plex. The door clicked behind her. She reached for it, but with a sinking heart, found it locked. Leaving was optional. Returning to the plex, Paul, and the life she'd always known wasn't. For better or worse, she'd made her choice. She only hoped it turned out to be a better one than the last time she'd said those words. Marion laid a protective hand over her flat belly and smiled.

The moon lit a circle of bare earth that surrounded the base of the plex. Beyond, the barren soil gave way to a sparse field, which grew thicker and then joined with trees. They looked so different from the ground, their bare trunks taller and thinner than she'd imagined.

She knelt, sifting raw, unsanitized dirt through her fingers.

The ruins she'd studied lay far beyond the shadow of the plexes. She started toward them. If people still lived out here, if the suicides were really those like her instead of those set upon death, they'd be there. Even if she had to make a go of it alone, she would. She'd read her history. She knew it would be hard, but it could be done. The tablet in her bag would tell her how.

Insects buzzed around her head and unruly plants made the ground uneven beneath her feet. She trudged onward, looking back only once. Tiny squares of light twinkled high above, but most of the apartments were dark.

Was Paul reporting her missing or had he gratefully accepted her departure and gone back to sleep? She only hoped he didn't suffer too badly from the social mistake of marrying her. She was a suicide. In a year, he'd be free to pick someone else. He'd given her the son she'd wanted, however unwittingly, and for that, she wished him well.

As for herself, she'd always belonged near the bottom of the plex. This was her place. She didn't need an ideal life, just the right to give one. Soon she would hold her son, and for however long he would share the world with her, she would be happy.

LEGACY

Five minutes out of the Dallas station, I couldn't take the chanting anymore. Balancing my purse and the gift for my grandson in one arm, I pried myself out from where I'd been wedged between a sweaty gentleman in a suit and a teen-aged waif that for all her skin and bones still managed to have more elbows than seemed humanly possible. I peered around the car and quickly spotted the source. A woman near the front of the train kept saying, "I believe," over and over.

Sitting alone three rows ahead, she wore a green dress, her short grey hair in well-manicured curls. She faced forward, rocking out of time with the rumbling cadence of the train. At first, I thought she was perhaps rocking a baby, like I was set to do later this afternoon, but then she raised both hands to pat down her hair. The rocking continued. So did the chanting, her voice just audible enough over the clacking of the wheels on the track to make my teeth grind together.

Maybe the poor woman wasn't quite right in the head. It wouldn't help matters to yell over several rows of people to ask her to pipe down. Surely, one of the attendants would see to her.

The threadbare navy blue cushion behind me offered a wan invitation, and the odor from the man by the window was even less enticing. The girl in the aisle seat worked a piece of gum in her mouth like it was the engine of the train itself. Six hours of this? We couldn't get to San Antonio fast enough.

A pair of female attendants made their way through the car, one pulling the shades along our side, where the morning sun was just beginning to reach maximum intensity. The other punched tickets while offering her usual sugar-coated smile. When they were only a few rows away, I wiggled back into my seat and set the box back on my knees. A quick search through my purse yielded my ticket.

As if seeing my ticket were some sort of warning light, the girl beside me began to pat down the many pockets of her blue jean jacket while the gentleman slipped one hand into his suit coat. He removed his ticket and proceeded to strangle it in a large fist much like a toddler with a slice of bread.

At least the idle chatter of the smiling attendant drowned out the chanting of the woman ahead of us.

The girl slid forward, her knees digging into the seat ahead of her as she squirmed around, driving her hands into her back pants pockets. With a relieved sigh, she came up victorious, her thrice folded ticket in her grasp. She settled back into her seat just as the attendant reached our row.

"Good afternoon," said the attendant. "Tickets please."

The girl unfolded hers and held it out. Punch.

The gentleman reached over me, driving his shoulder into mine as he leaned toward the aisle. The sleeve of his suit rubbed against me, emitting a strange rasping sound for what appeared to be tweed. The more I stared at it, trying to discern the cause of the sound, the color seemed to shift from grey to brown. I blinked, trying to clear my vision. My eyes weren't young and reading gave me trouble without my glasses, but colors hadn't ever bothered me before.

He all but waved the ticket in her face.

"Thank you, sir." Though her tone remained polite, her eyes narrowed and her smile lost its shine.

Punch.

He leaned back into his seat, allowing me room to breathe once again.

I held out my ticket.

Recognition flickered in her gaze. "Ah, Mrs. Hempleschmidt, how is your daughter doing?"

The gentleman stiffened.

The waify girl's gaze snapped to me.

The chanting grew louder. "I believe. I believe. I believe."

My skin started to tingle, the way it does when too much static builds up and you're just waiting for the shock to strike. Everyone seemed to be looking at me.

I cleared my throat with a cough and tried to ignore them. Was the fact that the attendant remembered me that shocking? I'd been riding the same train every other Saturday morning for the past several months, for goodness sake. Just because they weren't regulars didn't make me anything to stare at. How rude.

"She's doing well. Margaret had the baby last week. I'm bringing him a gift," I said.

I held up the box wrapped in light blue paper with white and yellow dots. The cramped seating arrangements were crushing the beautiful white ribbon bow. Not that little Isaac was going to care, but I wanted everything to be perfect for him. Margaret and her husband had tried so long for a baby and now he was here, a little miracle. Who knew what his future held, but in a matter of hours, he'd be holding the fluffy, white stuffed dog that the sales clerk had assured me would comfort Isaac for years to come. The first of many gifts from his Nana. His favorite Nana, if I had anything to say about it.

"That's wonderful. I'm sure we'll be seeing more of you then."

"I imagine so, unless Margaret gets sick of me."

The attendant laughed. "I'm sure she'll be happy for the help."

Punch. She returned my ticket and went on to the next row.

The woman in the seat in front of me spun around. "Isaac can't wait to see you. You're so important to him."

I gripped the box tightly. "How do you know his name?"

"Everyone knows his name. He sent me here to save you."

"Save me?" What was this madness?

Out of the corner of my eye, I thought I saw a bright flash of light to my right, but then there was nothing there other than the sweaty man in the suit. The air conditioning was running full blast in the car. How could he be that hot, even in a suit?

The woman vanished. Disappeared, just up and gone, like I'd imagined her for the last twenty minutes. Like she'd not just spoken to me.

I turned to ask the girl if she'd heard the woman, but she'd put on headphones and was busy mouthing lyrics between chomping on her gum.

That's when I noticed a handsome young man in an army uniform in the seat across the aisle. He smiled and nodded, as if agreeing with me, assuring me I wasn't crazy. He stood.

"Hurry. He's not supposed to be here." The uniformed man pointed to the man beside me. "Isaac won't develop the technology that shapes our future without you."

The man in the suit shuddered, gone for a second and then back, sitting and staring straight ahead as though nothing had just happened. I turned back to the young soldier, only to find he'd vanished.

"I believe. I believe. I believe," said the woman in green.

My heart started to pound in time with the chanting. What in the name of the Almighty was going on? I held on tighter to my purse.

Another man suddenly stood in the aisle beside the girl. "Mrs. Hempleschmidt, please come with me." He held out his hand.

"What is going on?" I shouldered my purse and gathered the box in one arm.

"We need to make sure you arrive in San Antonio like you did the first time. Your influence on Isaac puts him on the path we need."

"The first time?" Using the seat in front of me, I pulled myself to my feet.

"Quickly." He frantically waved me toward the aisle.

I didn't even get half a step before he was gone like the others.

No one else seemed to notice his disappearance. I started to call out to the attendants, but a different man from the front of the car came running at me in that same instant.

"Please, you must come with me. I only have-"

A ripple of energy moved through me as though I were being ripped apart, but a heartbeat later, the sensation passed.

And right there before my eyes, the man vanished mid-stride. I turned back to the girl and the gentleman. She had her eyes closed. He was staring straight ahead, his jaw muscles tight, one hand clamped down on the armrest by the window and the other tapping on his thigh.

In the next minute, each individual second lasted a lifetime. I stood there by my seat, gift and purse in hand, as seven more fellow passengers rushed at me, each begging for me to follow them, to get out of my seat, to get to the next car immediately. Each of them evaporated with a flash after speaking only a single sentence. The jarring super-speed flicker took over the suited man beside me. He was there, then gone again over and over. Each time a split-second shockwave passed through me.

Frozen, heart in my throat, I took in the empty seats that had been occupied when we'd left the station. No sign of those people remained. What did they want with me? I had to be losing my mind. None of this could be happening.

I took a deep breath. I'd taken this same trip many times. Nothing strange had ever happened. I wasn't anyone special, just one little boy's Nana.

The sunlight crept in around the edges of the pulled shades, casting beams of light throughout the car as we rocked along the track. Surely that had to be the flashing I kept seeing at the edge of my vision.

The flashing. The shockwaves. The man in the strange suit, who now stared at me with murder in his eyes. I needed help. Where were the friendly normal attendants who knew me?

I scanned the car for them, and only because I was doing so, saw seven more people blink away without a word. They barely got out of their seats before they were suddenly gone. With each flash, a jolt like an electric hiccup hit me. It was hard to breathe.

An elderly man approached me from behind, tapping me on the shoulder. I nearly jumped straight out of my skin. The box flew out of my hands and into the empty seat in front of me.

"Quick, you need the box," he said, his voice as shaky as I felt.

I shoved my way out, knocking into the girl's knees without thought for an 'excuse me' or manners of any sort. She scowled and muttered something under her breath.

"He doesn't belong here." The elderly man pointed an accusing finger at the suited man. "He has a bomb. He's going to kill you."

Free of the confines of my companions, I bent over the empty seat in the row ahead to reach for the box. "Why would anyone want to kill me?"

"Not everyone appreciates Issac's future."

Another shudder passed through the train. By the time I had the box back in hand and turned around, the elderly man was gone.

I was ready to scream.

The chanting changed, but the woman in green didn't turn around. I couldn't make out the words.

I grabbed the shoulder of a woman on the other side of the aisle. "What's she saying now?"

The woman, eyelids smeared with brown shadow and lips a shocking shade of coral, gave me the look I feared, like she had no idea what I was talking about, like I was indeed losing my mind.

"Does anyone else hear her?" I yelled, well past the point of caring if I caused a scene.

The few occupants left in the car, twelve in all, I noted as I spun around, hoping for some confirmation, shook their heads or whispered to those close by, all watching me. Why were they all watching me?

The clack clack clack of the train seemed to slow, each disruptive thunk and clank stretching out impossibly long for us to be still barreling onward toward San Antonio. It was as though we were underwater, but the sun still shone through the windows, illuminating dust motes in the shadows of the car.

"Mary Louise Hempleschmidt?"

The woman in green stood in the aisle, her hands braced on either seat beside her as she planted her sturdy black shoes on the worn blue carpet. Her face bore scars as did her neck. They appeared old and faded.

"Yes?"

"This bubble will only last a few moments. Please answer as quickly as possible." The woman peered past me. "Oh, I was so young."

I turned to see her gaze upon the girl with the earphones.

"No time for that now." She lifted her chin and inhaled loudly. "You've made the recording on the toy, yes?"

"How do you know about that?"

"Yes, or no?"

"Yes?" It was merely a quick little snippet, a few simple words my own mother had said to me as a child, a five-dollar add on for the toy. But I wanted Isaac to learn the sound of my voice, to know me. I'd visit on weekends, of course, but children grew so fast.

"Please hand me the box."

"It's only a toy that I'm going to give to my grandson. Nothing of great value." My purse slipped off my shoulder as I clutched the box to my chest.

She held out her hands. "You're wrong. This toy holds the words that shape the life of Isaac Pierson-Hempleschmidt. Words that shape our future."

I backed away until my feet hit the legs of the girl I'd been sitting with. She popped a big bubble in her gum. The snap made my nerves sing. Tears welled in my eyes and threatened to fall.

My voice trembled. "Help me."

"Isaac has demanded we make every effort to save you. Nineteen people have died trying. I will be the last, and I'm sorry, I can't save you. There have been too many attempts, too many slight changes. We're down to the last second of alterable time. That man," she pointed to the gentleman in the strange suit, "is from my time. His bomb injures all of us, but it kills you."

"Excuse me," grumbled the girl in long distended syllables, shoving her way past me with the slow-motion force of a dream. "I need to use the restroom." She got up, seemingly oblivious to the woman in green, and walked to the rear of the car.

"I'm sorry, Mrs. Hempleschmidt. Our projections have shown that if we can save the toy, it will offer suitable inspiration for Isaac to arrive at a future similar to the one we left. The words of a loved one are truly powerful."

It hardly felt so at the moment. My mouth hung open and it seemed I'd forgotten how to speak at all. I handed her the wrapped box, one corner dented and the paper torn. The ribbon bore a dirty streak and the bow was half flattened. A sad sight indeed.

The only sight of me my grandson would have if what this woman said was true. At least he would hear the recording.

"Thank you, Mrs. Hempleschmidt. Again, I'm so sorry."

She held the box reverently. "We only have a few seconds left, might I ask you for one small favor?"

I nodded, still dumbfounded but curious.

"I've heard Isaac say it so many times, but might I hear it from you? What you said to him?"

For an instant I again stood in the busy store, feeling silly talking into the quarter-sized button insert while I held the record tab. "Believe in yourself, and you can change the world."

She smiled and then the aisle was empty. The clacking of the train snapped back into full speed. I lost my balance. Confounded and confused, I reached for the seat and fell into it.

The man in the suit grabbed my arm.

Light flared as if all the shades had gone up at once. The shockwave hit again, knocking the breath from my body. A loud hot whoosh washed over me and I knew no more.

MRS. GILROY

"I can see your elevated pulse," Sharon said as she sat up, swinging her legs over the other side of the bed. "Another ship in from the fringe, I take it?"

Martin gave the back of her head an accusing glare. "You're not supposed to wear your gels to bed."

"Yes, well. I had a late shift last night and I'm on in..." She consulted the reader on her wrist. "Less than an hour."

He enjoyed the warmth of the blankets while she pulled on her grey med-tech uniform. It seemed like that was all she wore anymore. He hadn't even noticed the pale blue of the gels in her eyes when she'd come home last night. Could it be that he hadn't even looked at her during the few words they'd exchanged while she ate and he watched the news feed on the vid? His heart sank as he played back the hour between when she'd gotten home and when they'd gone to bed to lay side by side until sleep whisked them away.

"You work too much. We should take that vacation we've been talking about," he said.

"You mean the one *you* keep talking about?"

She went into the bathroom but left the door open. Somewhere in the four years they'd been married, they'd lost the need for privacy. He couldn't even hide his own pulse for goodness' sake.

Martin stared at the ceiling of their single-room unit on the lowly eighth floor of the plex. It was all they warranted. If he'd been fortunate to have a career like hers they'd be up higher, maybe with a window. They might even qualify for a second room and a child. It wasn't his fault the aptitude test had placed him as a docking bay assistant.

Or maybe it was. His instructors had always been after him to pay attention in class, but there was so much else to think about, so much more out there. Outside the plex, far from this five-generation-old colony, other humans were strewn throughout the known universe, living and working with creatures he'd only seen in newsfeeds.

The pristine white ceiling above, smooth and without flaws, acted as a canvas for his imagination. Far above this world, spaceships flew through the stars, darting from one planet to the next, their crews exploring, learning wondrous new things and meeting new beings. The hum of Martin's unit assigned maintenance bots became the ship's engines several decks below, barely audible in his suite.

"When are you on today?" Sharon called from the bathroom, shattering his daydream.

Not for several hours, but if he wanted to meet up with Arneco, it would have to be before his shift. Fringe ships only docked here long enough to unload and restock. Just another layover on their endless adventure. Talking to crewmembers on those ships was likely to be as close as he would ever get to exploring the wonders of the universe

"Soon. I'll walk with you." He got dressed.

She emerged from the bathroom. Her voice turned quiet and thick as she said, "Maybe you should just go."

"What? Go where?"

He fastened the last snap under his chin and turned to note that her olive skin was several shades lighter than usual. His hands dropped to his sides.

"Sharon, are you feeling all right?"

"No." She fussed with her sleeves until they fell exactly to her slender wrists. "You should go explore your heart out there." She pointed to the ceiling. "It isn't here."

The bones in his legs seemed to lose their solid form, depositing him on the edge of the bed with a heavy thump. His mouth went dry.

"What are you saying?"

"You may have fooled your instructors, but I know you're not dumb, Martin." Black hair swooshed over her shoulders as she shook her head. "I've put in for a release of our marriage contract. All you need to do is submit your authorization, and we'll both be free."

What was free? Alternating waves of panic and nausea wove throughout his body. He swallowed hard. He couldn't lose her.

She was all he'd wanted from the day he'd spotted her in the gardens at the top of the plex. Sunlight had sparkled on her dark hair, like tiny stars in a vast sea of deep space. Her intense gaze met his, full of mystery and intrigue. She'd smiled and he'd been drawn across the garden, heedless of the rows of fruits and vegetables standing between them, of the other occupants serving their community service hours, of the hoses and harvest bins. It had been a miracle that he hadn't tripped over anything, a testament that they were meant to be together.

He would be alone. If he authorized the release, he'd be back in a single rack unit. He'd have to box most of his things and he didn't have the funds to send them into expensive storage. He'd either be sleeping in half a rack with no room to roll over or he'd lose half of his belongings.

A soft ping sounded in his left ear, announcing a message from Arneco. His heart raced and his mouth went dry. Only being an assistant, he didn't warrant a full work interface like Sharon did. He needed to get to his station at the dock to read the message.

Sharon shook her head. "You're not even listening to me now, are you?"

"I am." He ignored the ping and the information it promised. "I'm right here, listening."

She huffed. "You're not."

Willing his legs to cooperate, Martin rose woodenly from the bed and took the six steps across the room to wrap his arms around her. "Tell me what's really wrong."

She was trembling, but she did return his embrace. "If I tell you, will you sign the release?"

"I'll think about it," he said hesitantly.

"Let's sit, shall we?"

She led the way into the dining table and took one of the two chairs. He sat across from her, annoyed that she'd put the table between them rather than sitting on the couch where they could be close.

"You asked how I was feeling."

Martin nodded.

"I haven't been well for the last few weeks. We ran some tests at work and it turns out I have an untreatable condition."

Now he was glad he was sitting down. "You have what? What's it called? How do they know it's untreatable?"

She exhaled loudly. "They're doctors, Martin. Trained professionals. They know what they're talking about. You wouldn't be able to pronounce the name of it anyway. It doesn't matter." She waved his barely uttered protest aside. "They've recommended that I go into stasis in the hopes that a cure will come to light in the future."

Black spots littered Martin's vision. Where was this coming from? Why hadn't she mentioned she'd not been feeling well? He couldn't lose her.

"Stasis? But surely not for a while. You seem fine. Can we at least enjoy some time together before then?"

Her gaze darted around the room before

coming to rest on him. "Today. They said today," she said. "I'm sorry, I meant to tell you a couple of weeks ago, but I wasn't ready. I've wasted too much time." She shook her head, her face resolute. "Stasis needs to be today so I have the best chance of surviving future treatment."

Sharon pushed herself away from the table and stood. "I'm trying to give you a way out, Martin. I don't know how long I'll be in stasis. It could be your entire life or longer. I'm doing you a favor. Get on one of those ships you've been dreaming about and start living your life." She smiled sweetly. "Do it for me."

His throat went dry. It took several deep breaths to force his voice to the same level of calm as hers. Falling apart would hardly instill confidence that he would stand by her, care for her like he'd promised to do in their contract. "I'll wait."

Her lips went tight, ironing out her smile in an instant. "Don't."

The nerves he'd forced out of his voice, broke free, cracking and wavering. "You really want me to go? To sign off on the contract? You don't want me to wait for you?"

"I'm asking you not to waste your life, waiting. I want you to be happy, Martin, and you would be happy somewhere else. Out there." She pointed at the ceiling.

The ping sounded again in his ear. Arneco must be getting impatient.

Though it broke his heart, agreeing rather than fighting was the kindest thing he could do for her. "If that's really what you want, I'll sign."

She walked over to him and leaned down to kiss his forehead. "Thank you, Martin. I'll have the contract sent to you shortly."

"Do you have to go into stasis today?" He rubbed his face, his eyes burning. "This is all so sudden."

"I'm sorry I didn't tell you right away. There never seemed to be a good time. I wasn't ready," she said. "We see these sudden types of illnesses all the time at work. I'm just glad we figured out what it was so quickly."

Thoughts of a future alone rained down all around him. "But what about your things? Our unit assignment? Can I visit you?"

Sharon clasped her hands before her. "My mother will get them for me. I'm not worried about any of that, and you shouldn't be either. As to visiting, sorry, no. I'll be in long-term storage after tomorrow, just one stasis tube in the midst of thousands in a warehouse. It's better that you remember me as I am now."

He nodded, a lump forming in his throat. This was the worst morning of his life. How could she be so positive? It was like this news barely affected her. Then again, she'd had time to process, to prepare. Maybe she was being strong for him.

"Can I be there when you go into the tube?"

"Of course. That might be good for you. Some closure, as it were."

He shook his head. Nothing could offer him closure, not today or a month from now. His mind refused to grasp what a day without her would be like. What would he do tomorrow? Tonight, in the bed alone?

His entire future had just turned to static.

"Come by on your break. We'll wait for you," she said.

"Is there anything I can do? Anything you need? Anything you'd like before you...?" There had to be something he could do.

"Just sign, Martin. I want to know you're free before I go in."

He nodded numbly, wishing he didn't have to go to work. He couldn't think straight, not after this. He was sure to mess something up and catch hell for it.

Martin forced himself to stand. He went to Sharon and held her, trying to memorize the feel of her in his arms. Her smell, the way her skin felt on his cheek, the taste of her lips.

"I'm going to be late," she whispered, her voice finally hinting at uncertainty.

He reluctantly let his wife go. The next time he saw her, she would no longer bear that title.

"I'll see you soon." Sharon gave him a tremulous smile and hurried out the door.

Martin went through his routine of getting ready for work on autopilot, his mind churning furiously to find some way to help Sharon. The spark of an idea flickered to life. Arneco.

He had two hours before his shift started, just enough time. Martin dashed out of their unit and headed toward the outer wall to the transport station. He boarded an upward-bound transport and arrived at the orbiting spaceport twenty minutes later.

A wide array of humanity rushed through the port with purpose, business meetings, customs, travel arrangements, stock transactions. It took him another ten minutes to get through the crowds to where Arneco's ship was docked. He approached the guard posted near the open ramp and requested his friend. A quick conversation on his com device brought the man down the ramp a few minutes later.

Arneco gave him a wink with his one good eye and a wide grin, showcasing his chipped front teeth. "There you are. I was beginning to wonder if you'd tired of my stories."

Martin forced a smile. "Not at all, but can we talk privately for a moment?"

When Arneco nodded, they moved a short way off. Away from the guard at the ramp and out of the bustling flow of the automated movers that were transferring the new load into one of the bays on the ship, Martin still couldn't manage more than a whisper. He glanced around one more time, not able to shake the sensation of Sharon looming right over his shoulder.

"There are doctors out on the fringe, right?"

Arneco nodded. "Why do you ask?"

"Good ones? Maybe with treatments we don't have here?"

"No laws against experimental treatments there," Arneco said. "Some of the best doctors head out to the fringe for what they call vacations. More like freedom to research for a few months, if you ask me."

"My wife is sick," Martin blurted. He swallowed and tried to regain his composure. "Something they can't treat here. I need to get her out there for treatment. Can you help me?"

Arneco chewed on his lower lip. "Passage to the fringe isn't cheap, my friend."

"She'll be cargo, in a stasis tube. I can take a single rack and work off some of the passage fee." Though the thought of being confined in that tiny space made his skin crawl.

"We can work that out, but we're leaving later today."

"Thank you. I'll be back with Sharon as soon as I can."

Arneco nodded. "Make it quick We're refueling now and cargo transfer will only take a few more hours. It will take time to get you logged in and your wife's tube stored securely."

For a second Martin put his problems aside and let his dreams soar. "How far away is the fringe?"

"Exactly seventeen jumps out this time around. Another year or two and we'll be at eighteen. We hope, anyway."

"Is it safe?" .

"Full disclosure here, friend." Arneco leaned in close. "Not all life forms are friendly, and I'm talking the ones both on and off the ship. Trade arrangements can go very wrong. Treaties are tenuous and broken over the slightest misunderstanding. There's a reason our ship is heavily armed and shielded. Even then, there are anomalies. Entire ships sometimes go missing."

The plex was safe. But Sharon needed this. They needed this.

It couldn't be all that bad. The ship Arneco worked on had a long docking record of traveling to the fringe and back. There were countless ships with histories even longer. People wouldn't continue to go out to the edges of the known universe if it were a terribly dangerous place.

Some of the most notable doctors had been out there for goodness' sake. They certainly wouldn't take chances with their important lives.

"We're going." Martin was rather surprised at how confident he sounded. And proud. Maybe it was the thought of seeing with his own eyes all the wondrous things he'd heard about from Arneco and others like him. Or was it that for once, he was going to be able to take care of Sharon rather than the other way around? He'd make sure she was cured. He'd do that, and then she'd be happy to sign another marriage contract with him. He could fix this.

"All right then." Arneco offered a smile and a nod and then started back toward his ship.

Heart pounding, Martin took stock of all he'd have to do to save his wife in the few hours he had before Arneco's ship left.

He sped back to this work station and pulled up the termination of marriage contract file Sharon had sent over. With halting strokes, he typed in his name in the three blanks and punched in his citizen code at the bottom to link his signature to the document. His stomach twisted as he forced his finger to click send. It was only a document. Only a step toward saving Sharon. Yet, every step he took as he walked away from his terminal left him feeling emptier than the one before.

"Where are you going?" asked one of his co-workers.

"I'll be right back." His voice lacked the conviction he'd had when talking to Arneco.

"Better watch it, the boss is on everyone today."

Martin's stride slowed. If he took off with Arneco, he'd lose his job. He only had a week of vacation, maybe two if he begged to use next year's allocation for this emergency situation. The trip out to the fringe was two months. One way.

This extended absence would mar his record permanently. He'd be stuck with temporary job placements, knowing he'd never hold a position of his own again, not even an entry-level one.

He needed to sit down. Sharon would have told him to take a deep breath and think this through. She would have told him to get back to his station and that she'd see him at lunch. At lunch...when she'd be going into stasis. Maybe for the rest of his life.

He had to get her to those fringe doctors. Once she was cured, the two of them could settle somewhere new, somewhere that didn't care about his records here.

He set off for the transport station at a pace just short of running. The downward shuttle seemed to take forever, as did the lift ride from the plex dock to their unit. He rushed inside.

Knowing they couldn't afford much cargo space, he packed them each a single bag. With the bags slung over his shoulder, he took a lift back to the upper floor transport station and tucked them away in a storage locker. The he hopped back on the lift.

Exiting on the twenty-seventh floor, a tastefully decorated mid-level zone of the plex that made their floor's lighting and furnishings seem harsh and plain, he made his way to the north quarter where Sharon worked.

He spotted her as he entered the clinic. She was talking to one of the doctors, smiling brightly, reminding him how she'd looked when they'd first been married. When had every day together become routine instead of and adventure? He sighed wistfully. Once she was cured, they'd start a new life out on the fringe, and out there, each day would be an adventure again. Even if they moved back a jump or two from the edge, found a colony in a safe place, there would always be jobs for med techs and people who knew their way around a dock. Maybe out there, the cost of living wouldn't be so high. They could find a nicer place than the bottom of the plex. The type of place that Sharon deserved with her standing, rather than the one she put up with for being with him.

"Hello, Martin," said one of Sharon's co-workers. "Let me get Sharon for you."

"I can-" he said, but she was already off across the clinic.

Sharon's eyes went wide. Her smile vanished as she raced toward him. "You're early. You did sign off on the contract, didn't you?"

"I did." He tried to sound relaxed so she wouldn't be suspicious. "You made it sound like the sooner you went into stasis, the better, so I talked to my boss and she gave me time off to see you now."

"To see me go into stasis, you mean," she said.

Martin nodded. "If you're ready." He took her hand. "This illness you have, if you're in there a long time, how will doctors know what you have so they can treat you in the future?"

The doctor she'd been talking to came over to join them. He stood beside Sharon. "It's good of you to be so concerned, really, but don't worry, we'll take good care of her. The stasis tube will contain a copy of her medical file."

"Good. That's good." As long as the fringe doctors had her information, they'd have what they needed to come up with a cure.

"We do have the tube ready." The doctor pointed to the metal cylinder nearby and then turned to Sharon. "You'll be quite comfortable.

I'll make sure of it."

"Shall we get started then?" asked Sharon. "No reason to wait, I suppose." She gave Martin's hand a squeeze and let go.

They followed the doctor over to the stasis tube.

"Are you sure I can't get you anything before you go in there?" Martin asked.

The tube didn't look all that comfortable. The padding at the bottom seemed thin and more plas than anything, probably cold and hard, a grungy grey color. The clearplaz on the top half seemed thick enough to withstand travel, but it still made him nervous. "What about power?"

"They have their own power, Martin. And a backup power system that can be used at any storage facility or during transport," she said.

"These tubes are made to withstand shipping, right? Where is this warehouse, anyway?"

Sharon came closer and patted his arm. "I told you, you don't need to worry about any of this. I'll be fine. Doctor Zapata will take care of everything. We ship these stasis tubes all over the known universe."

"They're as sturdy as any cargo container." Doctor Zapata smiled as he turned his gaze on Sharon. "After all, people are the most precious cargo, aren't they?"

Martin could only nod. His mind was too busy working on his plan.

Sharon took a few minutes to make the rounds to her coworkers, saying a quick farewell to each of them. When she came back to Martin, she took his hand.

"Promise me you'll take that trip out to the fringe."

"I'm leaving later today."

She grinned. "That's wonderful. I hope it's everything you've dreamed of."

"I hope so too."

Sharon leaned in and kissed him quickly. He tried to keep her there, to kiss her again, but she slipped away. Her coworkers drifted off, leaving the three of them next to the tube.

He shouldered Doctor Zapata aside to help Sharon onto the step halfway up the stand that the tube sat upon. She got one foot inside, then the other, and sat.

"Thank you, Martin. Now, go have your adventure." She patted his hand and then settled onto the pad, arranging her clothing to lie just right before resting her head on the thin pillow.

"One quick injection and then we're all set," said the doctor.

Martin stepped back, assured that there was nothing more for him to do.

The doctor administered the injection.

Sharon's eyes slipped closed and her face relaxed, lips curling into a slight smile. If he had to remember her, it would be like this, peaceful. However, he hoped to see her up and talking again in a few months.

Doctor Zapata sealed the tube, encasing Sharon in the safety of the thick clearplaz and metal. Nothing could possibly harm her until she was free of the tube once more. A wave of relief washed through him.

"Now that that's all settled, I'll take her to the transport station so she can be shuttled to the warehouse," said Martin

Doctor Zapata's eyes narrowed. "That's not necessary. We have a protocol for that."

"I'm sure you do, but she was my wife and as I'm going back to the dock anyway, it's one less thing you need to take care of. I'm sure you're a busy man."

"I suppose the tube is properly coded. It will get her where she needs to go." The doctor frowned as he made hurried notes on his datapad and beckoned an assistant over. He then returned his gaze to Martin. "You'll be careful with her?"

"Routing cargo is my job. You've done yours. Let me do mine." Though it bothered him to refer to Sharon as cargo, the way the doctor looked at her annoyed him even more.

Like the doctor would miss her more than he would? He was her husband for goodness' sake. Doctor Zapata had plenty of other med techs to assist him. Sharon was talented, but she wasn't irreplaceable, not to the doctor anyway. Not like she was to Martin.

He darted for the cart on which the stasis tube was mounted, elbowing aside Zapata's assistant. "If you want to help her, get busy finding a cure."

Martin pushed the tube out of the clinic and down the corridor filled with people. It took a while to make his way through, but he ended up cramming himself and the tube into a lift, leaving no room for anyone else. That didn't make the waiting crowds at each floor where the lift stopped very happy, but what did it matter? He would likely never see them again.

A lump formed in his throat as he imagined his future with Sharon, standing on an observation deck, watching the stars speed by, the fantastic bright nebulas, meeting strange beings. They would be side by side at the forefront of humanity, not locked away in an inside room on the eighth floor, going about their days in unending monotony.

He grabbed the bags from the locker at the transport station and wheeled the cart onto the next upward shuttle. He wished she were awake for the ride, but she'd see the stars eventually. Out at the fringe. When she was well again.

Martin arrived at his workstation with the stasis tube, out of breath and nerves singing. He sat on his stool, doing his best to appear like he was studiously working so no one would attempt to start up a conversation or assign him any additional tasks.

He'd had all of five minutes to cover his tracks in the system before his boss strode over with a scowl that was clear even in his peripheral vision. The moment he finished generating the shipping order for one female-occupied stasis tube on Arneco's ship, he looked up with a smile firmly in place. He nudged their bags further behind his station with his foot. "Can I help you?"

"You're late. Again."

"Actually, I was early. Ask Miguel if you don't believe me. I had to go retrieve this tube from the clinic to be shipped. Doctor Zapata sent a request."

Her shrewd gaze traveled from the tube to Miguel's work station. "I'd like to see this order." She held out her long, thin hand.

Martin tried not to let his own hand shake as he generated a hard copy of the order he'd just created and gave it to her.

She scanned the paper twice, top to

bottom. Martin began to sweat, sure he'd missed something.

"This is your wife?"

He nodded.

"I suppose I'll let it go this one time, but you hear me, Martin Gilroy, you've used up all your last warnings. There's a whole pool of young men eager for an entry-level job like yours, and you're certainly not advancing on my watch," she muttered as she walked away.

Her watch was about to end. Martin imagined all the things he wanted to say to her face, to scream at her, but none of that would help him slip away on Arneco's ship. Instead, he pressed his lips together tightly and retrieved the shipping order his boss had dropped to the floor upon her exit. After tucking their bags onto the bottom of the cart, he set out through the port with a light step despite his heavy load.

Arneco greeted him with a long low whistle. "I have to tell you, I didn't actually expect to see you here. I'm impressed. How did it go?"

Martin nodded to the stasis tube. "Quite well, considering. I hope we can find a cure for her out on the fringe."

"If anyone can, they will." He clapped Martin on the back and gave him a gentle push toward the loading ramp. "You'll have to put the tube with the cargo. I'm afraid the guest quarters are too small to accommodate it."

He could already feel the walls creeping closer. "It's a single rack, isn't it?"

"You expected anything else?"

At least Sharon would be in a large cargo bay and he could visit her there. He wouldn't be stuck in the rack other than to sleep. If his eyes were closed, he could pretend he was home in his bed with enough air to breathe, with room for his arms to stretch out beside him, that he could roll over without his shoulders rubbing the rack above him. *In through his nose, out through his mouth,* he repeated in his head. For Sharon, he could do this. To see his dream come true. He would do this. Martin pushed the tube ahead of him and into the belly of the ship.

Arneco led the way to the cargo hold where Martin watched as he fastened Sharon's tube against a wall using the straps and clips that lined the cavernous space. Crates, boxes, and cargo cubes were stacked in organized rows throughout the middle of the room.

"You sure have a lot of stock." It all looked so much more substantial in person. On screen it was just numbers and words. The shipments that were unloaded through the port must only be a fraction of what many of these ships actually carried. How many more ports, how many dockmen... His mind wandered as he considered it all. He realized Arneco was talking.

"We keep busy. Remember, everyone out there is reliant on what we bring until they can get their own colonies up and running. You have it damn good here. Fortunate, every one of you."

Martin shook his head. "Bored, every one of us."

Arneco chuckled. "You'll need to see the stockman to pay for passage and file your documents."

"Right." Martin shivered. His palms began to sweat. He had been saving credits to give Sharon a pleasure cruise, but he didn't yet have enough for them to even get to any worthy destination, let alone afford return passage.

She wanted him to follow his dream. His dream included her and that couldn't happen in the plex.

"I need access to a terminal to get my payment in order. This was a bit of a rush with Sharon's illness and all."

Arneco brought him up a level on a set of narrow metal stairs. The ship seemed larger inside, longer, filled with so many small spaces. He opened a narrow door to a room just big enough for a stool and a plain black vid screen with a terminal worn smooth by the dancing of thousands of fingers. "You can use this public terminal. Best to do it now while we're at the port and it's free. Once we're out in space, the rates are astronomical."

"Thanks." Martin slipped inside and situated himself on the stool, his knees banging into the table legs for lack of anywhere else to be.

Arneco closed the clearplaz door and leaned against the wall beside it. Knowing he was waiting, Martin quickly logged on and accessed his account. He opened the silver canister next to the terminal and shook out a blank credit chip. Its edges were dented and all hint of color had been rubbed from its tarnished grey surface. How many others had transferred their savings onto this same chip to hand to the stockman?

He inserted it into the port and drained his personal account of all the credits he'd saved. Then he took a deep breath and emptied the joint account that supplied them with meals, their clothing allowance, and their living unit. It still wasn't enough. He emptied Sharon's personal account too. Her health and their future were worth it. She would understand. He hoped.

His hands shook as he ejected the chip and clutched their entire worth to his chest. Martin opened the door.

"All set?"

Martin nodded.

"I've been informed there's a Doctor Zapata ranting at our door, something about the stasis tube belonging to him? A shipping statement error?"

"It might be his stasis tube, but she's my wife. He wanted to send her off to long-term storage. Why would he be looking for her now, anyway?"

Arneco shrugged. "Seems quite upset, if you ask me. He's her personal doctor?"

"They work together. Did he say something was wrong with the tube or Sharon?"

"No. Just that there was a routing error."

"He couldn't cure her. She's no longer his concern." He had half a mind to find his way back to the loading ramp and do more than elbow the doctor aside this time. But he needed to make his payment, and the ship was almost ready to launch.

"I'll send him off then." Arneco tapped his com device and relayed the statement. "Let's get our tour underway. I'll be needed elsewhere shortly."

They walked through the corridors, Arneco pointing out where to take meals, the single racks where he and the other few passengers would be bunking, and the couple rooms they used for entertainment. It wasn't as much space as Martin had hoped. Most of the ship was dedicated to stock, and he wasn't allowed in any of the secured areas. They paused at a terminal where Martin had to enter his personal information and both a hand and retinal scan. After a few minutes, Arneco generated a passcard. He handed Martin a thin chip on a strap.

"This will allow you access to your rack and the other public rooms. I've also keyed it to the storeroom where your wife is. I know I'd want to check on her if she were mine."

Martin slipped the strap around his neck and tucked the card under his shirt.

"You'll be tracked so be sure to only touch what belongs to you. The card will get you two meals a day. Keep your credit chip close and don't gamble." He rolled his fat lower lip up into the thick mustache that covered most of the upper one. "I'm warning you. The crew will take you for everything you've got, and I'm guessing you don't have anything to lose."

"True." Being perpetually monitored wasn't anything new. Everything in the plex was tracked too. Tracked and charged to his account. The account that now resided on the chip clutched in his hand that would contain next to nothing when they arrived out on the fringe.

They went to see the stockman to log his

payment. A tall man with a thin face and thick billowing tufts of white above his eyes held out his hand.

Martin handed over their life savings.

The stockman inserted Martin's chip and huffed. "This is all you have?"

"It's enough," said Martin, sure of the number Arneco had quoted.

The stockman looked down his long nose at Martin. "What about when you get to your destination?"

"Is it possible," Martin cleared his throat, "to find employment during passage?"

The stockman looked him over. "Your file says you worked on the docks."

Martin nodded. "Mid-level clearance."

"We have plenty of dock workers."

But that's what he did. It was a useful skill. How could they not need him? "Is there anything you do need?"

"Do you know how to service maintenance bots?"

Was this a test or a joke? Everything in the plex was automated on that level. Surely a ship like this had the same level of technology. Martin forced a grin. "You must have a repair bot for that?"

"I wouldn't be asking if we did. I take that as a no?"

"Kitchen help perhaps?"

"I don't think so. You'll have better luck on the fringe. They're always looking for entry-level workers."

"Because there are so many jobs?" Martin asked.

"Because the mortality rate is so high. The fringe is a dangerous place. Best of luck to you when you get there." The stockman smiled thinly. He dismissed Martin with a jut of his chin.

Martin shoved the credit chip into his pocket and spun around to ask Arneco for help, but he was gone. The walls pressed in closer. Martin nearly tripped over his own feet in his rush to the door. It took him an hour of wandering to find his way back to his rack. The long corridor was mostly empty as he counted his way down to the narrow enclosed rectangle on the top row. The rungs of the ladder dug into the soft soles of his shoes. He tried not to think about how many hands had touched the same rungs as he climbed to his third-row rack. At least at the top, he wouldn't have anyone climbing past his entry slot. When he'd been there with Arneco, he'd tossed his belongings inside and continued on his tour. Now there was no one waiting to distract him from the fact that his entire personal space had shrunk from a full unit with multiple rooms in the plex to a space barely half as wide as the bed he'd shared with Sharon and just tall enough for him to sit up in.

After arranging the little he'd packed on the two shelves at the foot of his rack, he settled onto his back on the thin mattress. It was a far cry from the comfort of the bed he'd shared with Sharon. Pulling the curtain closed over the entry slot near the middle of his rack, he attempted to convince himself that he was home in his bed with Sharon sleeping beside him. The soft sound of her breathing would help him drift off to sleep. Could he sleep for months and just wake up on the fringe?

Maybe he should have figured out how to get himself into a stasis tube, travel expenses would have been cheaper. But it wasn't like stasis tubes were sitting around the plex for anyone and everyone to use. The medical staff wouldn't have given him one unless Sharon had convinced them to, and that would have meant telling her about his plan.

The plan that he'd thrown together. The plan she wasn't going to like. Not at first, anyway. Once she understood why he'd done it, she'd thank him.

She would. Wouldn't she? His eyes sprang open. The dim light through the curtain was more than enough to remind him of where he really was. To remind him where she was. Alone in the storage bay, her tube strapped to a wall along with a room full of merchandise. At least he could go see her every day. It would give him plenty of time to figure out how to evade Sharon's wrath when she woke up.

Feeling slightly more at ease, he breathed in through his mouth and out through his nose. That didn't help make the space feel any larger. The ceiling hung right over him, within reach, and it wasn't the pristine white of home. Black scrapes marred the smooth grey metal surface. And the walls. The bottom of the curtain was frayed. Rather than speculate how many others had been in this rack or how often they were cleaned by the questionably operational cleaning bots, he decided he needed to calm his mind a bit more before attempting sleep. A walk would help, one without Arneco's rapid commentary or worrying about meeting the stockman. That was over and done, his situation clear, even if it was bleaker than he'd wanted. This was for Sharon. They'd make due, figure things out once she got well.

Arneco had mentioned an observation deck. Without anywhere else to be, Martin took his time, retracing the tour he'd taken until he came to the closed door with the sign beside it written in common Trade to let him know he'd arrived at the correct place. Fishing the passcard out of his shirt, he swiped it through the reader. The lock clicked and then the door slid open.

He'd always imagined staring out a window on a spaceship would be a glorious experience. A breath-taking expansive view to be savored from the comfort of an elegant chair or perhaps leaning against a polished prism glass railing. Sharon would be beside him, laughing, talking, smiling. They might even be sipping wine or liquor from some far-off world, a luxury they couldn't afford in the plex.

Martin swallowed hard. None of that would happen here.

The observation deck was nothing more than a square room outfitted with a ceiling-sized vid that projected the view outside. There were no chairs, no ship staff to ask if he needed anything, no hint of any luxury at all. It wasn't even the real view of space. He slumped down onto the floor and laid back to stare upward, trying to convince himself this was better than sitting in a comfortable chair back home, watching the vids as he skimmed the datapool while Sharon sat beside him studying some new disease or treatment.

If he tried not to think about it, he could imagine that the vid was the real view outside, but then his nose twitched and he sneezed.

Glancing around the room, he noticed trash in the corners and dust on the floor. Maybe the stockman hadn't been messing with him. Maybe they really didn't have reliable maintenance bots. Nothing here was white or clean. The ship made even his plain eighth-floor unit seem pristine and elegant.

Martin wiped at his uniform, brushing off the dust. He didn't have many changes of clothing. He'd have to make his limited wardrobe last until they arrived.

Traveling to the fringe was supposed to be a grand adventure, he reminded himself. Even if it wasn't exactly as grand as he'd envisioned, this was the dream Sharon had encouraged him to pursue. She knew how badly he wanted this and now he was here, doing the one thing he'd desired since he was a child. All those years of skimming the feeds for images and rumors, his imagination gorging on the sumptuous meal. He glanced at the projected stars once more before heading back to his rack where he crawled inside and slept.

Martin spent his days standing below the observation vid. He watched the first deep-space gate with awe, the approach seemed to take hours. The ring had grown from a single star-looking dot to a loop large enough for two freighters side by side.

The gate floated in blackness with nothing remarkable within view to mark its location. His pulse raced as the ship slipped into the ring.

It was all over in the blink of an eye. One moment they were passing into the ring and the next, they popped out of an exact duplicate in another well of black space. He stared at the vid, waiting for something remarkable to happen, something to indicate the massive amounts of space they'd just skipped over, flashing lights, clanging warning bells, an announcement, something. But they merely traveled onward.

When they reached the first port, he observed the station which orbited a blue-green world with barely-contained glee. Three other ships were also docked. He ran down to the bay to wait for the doors to open.

Crewmen bustled around him, preparing crates and containers for offloading. So this was what it looked like inside the thousands of ships that had passed through the dock where he worked.

"Do you need help with that?" Martin asked the closest person.

The woman shooed him aside. "You'll need to wait over there, out of the way."

Like he was useless. He wasn't. Martin sighed and went to wait against the wall. When the bay doors finally opened, he bolted down the ramp. Unlike the docks where he worked, there were no shouted orders bouncing around the giant open space that formed the tunnel-like outer ring of the port, no crews of uniformed workers waiting to inventory the incoming items.

An old man with a long grey beard sat at the desk in the center of the room. He looked Martin's way long enough to note that he carried nothing before turning his attention back to the crew coming down the ramp with their loaders stacked high.

Martin drifted away, passing through the main chamber and into the halls. The design was similar to the port where he worked, but wear was evident on every dented wall and scuffed floor. Graffiti covered the three-story wall that opened up in the middle of the station—layers upon layers of paint, a cacophony of color that made it painful to attempt to pick out any single image.

He wandered to where the market should have been, but there were only empty stalls and children peering at him over the half walls that divided the area. Their hair was long and unwashed, faces smeared with dirt. No parents lingered about. No strange alien creatures. No exotic wares that made him wish he had credits to spend.

Martin walked for another hour, searching for the wonders he'd dreamed about, but only found poor people living on a port falling into disrepair. Stomach swimming with emptiness, he returned to the ship and to his rack and slept.

As they traveled, he ate as little as possible, saving his ship credit for the day he was ready to wake Sharon. She would need to eat too. Her waking would have to wait until they were close to the fringe so that they both didn't starve.

They passed through eight more rings over the next two weeks. From his self-imposed station under the vid, he observed planets, some swirling in color like an artist's discarded pallet and others merely subdued shades of grey or yellow. Sometimes they were close enough he could spot their moons. Most remained at a distance, probably something to do with those tenuous treaties Arneco had mentioned. They passed by translucent nebulas dancing with golden hues. He locked the memories away to share with Sharon.

At the next port, Martin hung back, waiting until they had fully docked before slipping out. He went directly to the market to see if this port was more prosperous than the last. There he found four vendors, all on opposite corners of the marketplace. None of them were human. Upon his arrival, a grey-skinned creature with dangling eye stalks began gesturing wildly with his seemingly boneless arms. In another corner, a blue thing with squid-like tentacles shrieked something repeatedly at a near eardrum-rupturing pitch. Someone grabbed his arm and yanked him away from the market.

"We're not supposed to be in there," said Arneco. He pointed to the sign beside the entryway.

Martin scanned the various lines of characters until he found one he could read. "No humans? Why?"

"One stole something here. Once. Doesn't take much to break trust. Watch the signs. We can't afford an incident that could result in getting us banned from the port."

"But they need you."

"There are other supply ships." Arneco led him toward a food dispenser.

"I don't have any off-ship credits," said Martin.

Arneco waved off his concern. "I've got this." He ordered two meals.

The machine flashed inside, emitting a low grinding noise. A heavy thunk and several minutes later, the lower door opened to reveal two bowls full of a steaming green substance.

"What is that?"

"Better you don't know. It tastes kind of

like creamed spinach." He handed a bowl to Martin and grabbed utensils from the wall-mounted bin next to the dispenser. They headed for a nearby table.

Martin sat across from Arneco. "Why are these ports in such bad shape? That dispenser must be over seventy years old.

"These ports are old. The new ones are out by the fringe."

"So they just fall to ruin once they're built?"

Arneco made quick work of his bowl of green mush. "Out here you learn to repair it yourself or live with the state it's in.

Martin caught himself longing for the clean surfaces and routinely updated equipment of the plex. He finished the glop in his bowl and tried not to think about the fresh meals he was missing at home.

They returned to the ship and barely stepped aboard when sirens blared.

A harried female voice boomed over the speakers, "A riot has overrun the port. Everyone to their stations for an emergency departure."

Booming noises thundered through the walls as the hatch doors slammed shut. Martin wondered if the other passengers had made it back inside.

The engines fired up, filling the recent silence with their familiar hum. Alone and unneeded in dealing with the emergency, Martin made his way to Sharon.

The ship shook as it disengaged from the docking clamps and then glided onward as usual. He stood next to the stasis chamber, peering inside. Were they close enough? His heart ached for her voice, her real voice, not the one he imagined. And her touch. Martin bit his lip. Maybe he'd wake her tomorrow.

Arneco found him there hours later. "We've received reports that our last scheduled stop has been invaded by a species with which we have no treaties. They're also controlling our next gate. We're going to have to take an uncharted detour." He clapped Martin on the shoulder. "That's what you've been waiting for, right? Some excitement?"

He forced a grin.

"You should return to your rack. It might be a bumpy ride."

Martin nodded and watched Arneco leave. He much preferred the openness of the storage bay, but with all the heavy supplies here, it could quickly become a dangerous place for a soft-fleshed being. Alone in the rack, he'd have nothing to do but wonder what was going on. Instead, he went to the observation room, where he could at least see what was happening.

Hours passed in a blur of stars as he lay

alone on the floor. Half-asleep, he imagined Sharon there with him. But instead of lying back and enjoying the view, she berated him for selling their home, for spending every last one of their credits, and losing all their belongings.

"We'll get new ones," he told her.

"We're broke. You've ruined us."

"You need a better doctor. We can find one out here."

Her eye narrowed and she sprang to her feet. "This isn't the plex, Martin. You've seen these people and how things work differently out here. Medical care isn't a free benefit. Just how do you plan on paying a doctor?"

His heart thudded and his throat went dry. How dare she throw his darkest realization right in his face? "We'll figure it out. You're my wife. We signed a contract to take care of one another," he told her as he stared at a tiny blue planet.

"We both voided that contract. I'm not your wife anymore. I told you to leave, to be happy. This is your dream, not mine."

He wished he could touch her, but knew she would vanish if he did. "I can't be happy without you, don't you understand? They can cure you out here. It will all work out. I promise."

Sharon's glare pierced him straight through. "You've ruined us. Spent every credit we had."

"I had to. For you."

"Martin, you've lost your mind! No one will treat me for free. I'm as good as dead."

He sat up, wrapping his arms around himself. "Don't say that. We'll figure something out."

When he could make himself meet Sharon's angry glare again, he was both relieved and distraught to see she'd vanished.

Shapes appeared on the screen overhead. The ships were much bigger than the one he was on. A gate floated in the distance. Martin got to his feet, as if being that much closer to the ceiling would help him reach the ring faster.

One of the ships drifted closer, yellow beams of light shooting outward, racing toward the freighter. Orange dashes raced from the freighter toward the oncoming ship. The walls shook around him. Alarms activated, filling the room with loud clanging and flashing lights. A booming voice announced that the emergency seals were in place. He clamped his hands over his ears.

A narrow white flash of light raced toward the ship, coming right for him. Martin clenched his teeth and hunkered low, but he couldn't tear his gaze from the view above. Light flashed through the ship, through the observation room, through Martin himself. Energy flooded his body, jolting him stiff until his lungs screamed for his next breath. Paralyzed, he fell onto the floor. The light washed through him, the room and then through the wall inward. And then he could breathe again.

The screen overhead flickered, its intermittent projection revealing that Sharon had returned. Every muscle ached as he got to his knees.

"Don't worry," he told her. "We're close now. We'll reach the gate and the next thing you know, we'll be at the fringe. We'll find a doctor, get you healed. Then we can get new jobs, start a new life. You'll see. We'll be fine. We'll be better."

She squatted in front of him. After fussing with her sleeves, she scowled. "We're going to die here."

"No. We're so close. Arneco won't let anything happen to us."

"Arneco is just one man. An employee on this ship, who likes to tell grand stories. You notice that none of the things he told you have been true so far?"

"He did say it was dangerous. That's true."

Sharon slapped him. "And you brought me here anyway."

He expected his face to sting, but he just felt cold and hollow. "He couldn't have been lying about everything."

"Like how he said there were hostile alien races?"

"Yes," he whispered.

The ring loomed over the ship. They must have been speeding forward faster than they'd traveled before to reach it so quickly. Yellow light flashed all around, pulsing over the flickering screen. The walls shuddered with an ominous metallic thunder, interrupted by the shattering sound of an immense explosion. Martin flew backward, hitting the wall with such force that black dots closed in on his vision, wavering in and out of view. He gasped as pain blossomed up and down his spine.

The ring passed overhead and then there was only deep blackness dotted with distant stars on the screen above. Sharon sat beside him. The screen flickered one last time and went black.

"You're all alone now." She said in a flat voice that made him cringe both inside and out. "The rest of the ship is gone. You heard it explode. My body is gone. You've killed me, Martin."

Nausea overwhelmed him. He heaved his meager last meal onto the floor.

Wiping his mouth on his sleeve, he got his stomach and nerves back under control. "If the rest of the ship is gone, why is there still air?"

Sharon shrugged. "Probably won't last long."

"You're wrong." He couldn't make it this close to the fringe to die without ever seeing it. He couldn't.

Martin got to his feet, his legs shaking beneath him. He headed for the door.

"What are you doing?" Sharon shrieked. "You can't open that. You'll die."

He palmed the pad. The door opened.

The sirens clanged. The dim emergency lights did a poor job of lighting the hallway, but it was still there.

"See," he said, without turning around. "Everything is fine."

"The seals were closed. You heard the announcement. You open the sealed door, and you'll find yourself floating in space."

He took one step and then another. Arneco had said this freighter was heavily armored. It was built for this sort of thing. He wasn't about to sit there in the dark, waiting to take his last breath. He'd risked everything, dammit. He was going to see Sharon alive and well again and he was going to see the edge of the known universe before that breath came.

Martin left Sharon's angry specter behind and sought out the door that sealed off the corridor he'd traveled so many times. The sirens suddenly went silent. The muffled sound of a distant ship-wide announcement caught his attention, but he couldn't make out the words.

If there was an announcement, there had to be someone there to make it. The ship and Sharon's stasis tube had to still be there.

Heart pounding, Martin palmed the pad.

The door opened to a bright corridor. He stepped through. The door closed behind him. He'd barely taken twenty steps before two men came running toward him, their eyes intent and jaws set, weapons in their hands. He hurried out of their way.

"What do you think came through?" one said to the other.

"No idea, but it's going to die." The second man slowed, his stunner held steady as he scanned the corridor.

If something had boarded the ship behind him, the last place he wanted to be was between the creature and the men hunting it. He rushed onward until he reached the other passengers climbing out of their racks.

"What's happening?" he asked one of them.

The woman didn't answer despite the fact that she was walking straight toward him. And she didn't slow down. Before Martin could dodge out of her path, she walked right through him.

Martin stood there, shivering at the utterly uncomfortable feeling of another body moving through his own. If he'd had anything left in his stomach, he would have purged it right there.

He didn't remember dying, and he wasn't a damn ghost. Martin spun around trying to find someone who could see him, but the others were busy packing up their belongings.

"Where are you all going?" he asked.

The other passengers quietly gathered up their bags and milled about as if waiting for something.

Arneco arrived moments later. "Good, you're all ready. The other ship will be joining up with us momentarily. It will be cramped but safer for all of you while we attempt to understand what happened to the missing section of our ship. Any personal cargo will be transferred as well. They only have one more gate and then you'll be at your destination. Now, if you'll please follow me."

Martin held out his hands. He could see himself just as well as anyone else.

He followed the others as they made their way to a much smaller bay than the one they used when docking at stations. A simple round doorway served as the opening through which four men in clean white singlesuits entered.

"These are the passengers?"

"Yes," said Arneco. He pulled a datapad from his pocket and glanced between it and the passengers. "We seem to be missing one. Has anyone seen Martin Gilroy?"

The passengers looked at one another and shook their heads.

"He wasn't with you in the racks during the attack?"

"Didn't see him," one of them said.

"Spent most of his time in that observation room," said another.

Arneco bowed his head. "If he was in there during the attack...that whole section was phased."

"Carl will try to recover that section for you," said one of the white-suited men. "But to be honest, we've only encountered a partial ship phasing once before. We're not sure how to reset the molecules to realign them with our reality."

Arneco nodded. "Carl said it was dangerous, but the captain wants to try before we make the call to abandon ship. We've got another freighter on call for the rest of the cargo and the crew."

"Could lose the whole thing," he said. "If you ask me, Carl's a bit nuts for volunteering for this."

The other three white suits ushered the passengers through the round door and into the flexible connection tubing that led to their ship.

Martin watched the others leave while Arneco talked with the other man. He wasn't dead, he was simply out of phase. He choked on his own crazed laughter.

All personal cargo would be transferred. Sharon.

He couldn't leave her and he didn't want to become a puddle of goo or blinked straight out of existence. Martin followed the other passengers.

Cramped was not an adequate word for the the other ship. As all of their cargo was transferred to a tiny bay already filled with the ship's own load, the few unoccupied racks were snatched up by the new passengers. Martin found very little space to stand where he wasn't passed through. The sickening sensation did not seem to lessen with each occurrence. If anything, he felt worse, drained and tired.

The last item they loaded aboard was Sharon's stasis chamber. Arneco rolled her into the overflowing bay and spoke to the white-suit who was logging all the new cargo.

"Have your doctor look over her records. Her husband was seeking treatment for her out here. Maybe your doctor can get her to the right people."

The woman nodded, eyeing the chamber with a raised eyebrow.

"I'll transfer over what little was left in her husband's account, but make her a good offer on the chamber. She'll need the credits," Arneco said.

"I'll see to it."

"And when she asks about her husband, give her my condolences."

The woman nodded.

Arneco took one last look at the chamber and then departed.

After the last of the cargo had been loaded and everyone was crammed aboard, the ship detached. Martin stood beside the stasis chamber until one of the other crewmembers came over and spoke to the woman. She pointed him toward Sharon.

"Let's see what we have here." The man activated the screen on the side of the tube where Doctor Zapata had indicated Sharon's medical records would be stored.

This doctor rubbed his chin and glanced around at the milling faces. He shook his head and sighed heavily.

Was she truly incurable? Had they traveled all this way for nothing? Martin held his breath, watching the doctor's every movement.

"I can't wait to hear this one," he muttered to himself as his fingers tapped rapidly over the controls.

The light inside the stasis chamber came on, and after a few moments, there was a loud click. A gap appeared between the two halves of the chamber.

He was waking Sharon now? "We're not at the fringe yet! What are you doing? Every minute she has between now and treatment is precious."

But no one could hear him. Martin tried to push the top half back down, to find a button to seal the tube again. But nothing he did influenced the reality around him.

Martin's heart leapt as Sharon's eyes fluttered open. She sat up slowly and blinked as if trying to clear her vision. "Where is Doctor Zapata? He promised he'd be here when I woke up."

Why would he promise that if she was going into long-term storage? Martin crowded in as close as he dared without touching either of them.

"Ma'am, where was this Doctor Zapata supposed to wake you?" asked the doctor.

"In the clinic. He said I'd only sleep for a..." Her gaze darted around the room. "Where am I? Where's Keith?" Her voice grew more frantic by the second. "Tell me what's going on. Tell me right now!"

Her words bounced around in his head

until they began to fall flat, deflated and hollow. Panic at waking up here without him was understandable, but why was she expecting to be in her clinic with Doctor Zapata? She'd never called him Keith at home. The hollowness sunk to his stomach.

"Take it easy, ma'am. You need a few hours for your body to adjust after months in stasis."

"Months? Keith! Someone get me Doctor Zapata. Immediately. He's got some explaining to do."

Keith? What about himself? Martin's entire body went tight, hands forming fists. Doctor Zapata wasn't the only one with explaining to do. She'd faked her illness to leave him? For *Keith*?

"Ma'am, you should stay seated."

Sharon pulled herself up despite the doctor's warnings. She swung a leg over the side of the tube. "Help me down. Where the hell am I?"

"Your ship ran into an issue, and you've been transferred here."

"My ship? I shouldn't be on a ship." Her hands shook where she held onto the side of the tank.

"We'll be at the fringe within a couple of hours. You should rest until then."

Her face blanched. "The fringe? No." She

sagged against the tube.

The doctor grabbed her arm, propping Sharon up beside him. "I'm afraid there's been an incident. I'm sorry to inform you that your husband has perished."

"I have not," Martin said, even though he knew no one could hear him.

"Well, that's just great." She rubbed her face with her free hand. "I think I'd like to sit down now."

The doctor nodded. He half-carried Sharon over to a storage container and helped her to sit down on it.

It was great he was dead? Martin slammed his fist through the stasis chamber to no effect.

"You do realize there are legal implications for frivolous use of a stasis tube?"

Frivolous indeed. She wasn't sick. All of this had been for nothing. Martin slumped to the floor, heedless of the milling people that walked through him.

"It wasn't exactly frivolous," Sharon said. "Martin had a kind heart. I didn't want to hurt him. Using the tube for a day seemed like the best answer to allowing both of us to be happy." She peered around the room with tears welling in her eyes. "The stasis tube wasn't supposed to leave the clinic. I'm not supposed to be here."

The doctor patted her arm. "I suppose I

could take the tube off your hands and make that bit of a mess go away?"

Sharon looked right through Martin to where the tube sat. She wiped her eyes with the back of her hand, and then as if she could see her reflection, went about putting her hair to rights. Once she was finished smoothing it all into place, she sat up straight and turned to the doctor. "I suppose all sorts of things disappear out here? Drop out of legal sight?"

He didn't indicate any sort of answer but did pull a datapad from his pocket. After he'd typed on it for a moment, he handed it to Sharon.

"Here's my offer. It's not enough to get you back to the registered location of that tube, but if you work here for a year or two, you could probably manage it."

"A year. Or two. Here."

Martin sat watching her, this woman he'd lived with for four years, as though she were a stranger. The light he'd loved in her eyes had dimmed. Her hair no longer gleamed with silken mystery. Her skin didn't call to him, begging to be touched. She was someone else now. Someone else's now.

But probably not Keith's.

Laughter bubbled up inside. No wonder Zapata had been so upset to find Sharon's tube logged into Arneco's ship. For the first time, knowing no one could hear him was a benefit. He let the laughter spill out until tears rolled down his face and the humor had turned sour.

Sharon nodded. "Transfer the credits. I'd hope I have an account chip here somewhere."

"Your bags are on the cart below the tube."

She walked past Martin and rummaged through both of their bags. "There's nothing in here. Where the hell are my credits? Martin couldn't have spent everything. He wouldn't have, not if he thought he was coming out here to find treatment for me."

"Perhaps he had the chip on him?" the doctor said.

Martin stroked the credit chip still in his pocket. He couldn't give it to her if he wanted to. He wasn't entirely sure that he was sad about that either.

Sharon's lips drew tight and she exhaled loudly. "I don't suppose you would assist me with setting up a new account here?"

"For a small fee."

She nodded. "I figured as much. And sending a message home?"

"If you wish." He consulted his datapad again. "Arrival is estimated at six to eight weeks. Your news will still be valid at that time?"

"It will be years before I can go home according to you, but yes, news that I'm alive will hopefully still be valid. My mother will be sick with worry. Keith too, I would imagine."

Martin half-hoped Keith was busy eying one of his other assistants by now, but maybe he did genuinely care about Sharon. But to wait years for her? That seemed unlikely.

The doctor shrugged. "There will also be a fee for the message."

"Of course there is."

"I'll get a new chip set up for you and then we'll work on that message. We should be at the last port in eight to nine hours. You'll want to be rested up and ready to hit the ground running by then."

"I'm not sure I like the sound of that. Where do I go? What do I do? I've never even considered coming out here."

"Sorry, I'm not a tour guide," he snapped. "I have to stay with the ship. You'll have to find your own way. Stay with the stasis tube until I return."

The doctor wove between the passengers and then was gone from sight. Martin struggled to get to his feet, his strength waning with every breath. Had he left a part of himself on Arneco's ship? He'd been weak there after leaving the observation room, but nothing like this. He held up his hand, half expecting it to be transparent, like he was some sort of ghost. But it was just his own trembling hand, pale and clammy. Martin decided it might be best if he rested awhile too.

Except Sharon didn't rest. She smiled and talked to the other passengers until she managed to borrow a datapad from one of them. She stood beside Martin, leaning against the stasis tube, fingers flying over the screen as she took in as much information about their destination as she could find.

Martin smiled. She was a capable woman. She'd make her way out here just fine. Just like he knew she would. Although, he'd envisioned himself beside her in a more solid form when he'd set out on this journey. A form that didn't feel like it's every fiber was being slowly pulled to a distant location.

He must have drifted off because he found himself sprawled on the floor with Sharon standing in his legs talking to the ship's doctor. Martin shook his head, attempting to clear the heavy fog that seemed to be holding him back from the reality where everyone else was. Sharon's voice was muffled and the words made little sense. After a few minutes, she went to an empty chair with the doctor's datapad and sat down. She talked to the pad for a few minutes, her face forlorn.

By the time Martin was able to summon enough energy to stand, the fog had cleared enough that he could hear clearly again, though everything sounded distant.

Sharon handed the datapad back to the doctor. "Thank you for sending the message for me."

"I've already deducted the fees we discussed." He dropped a credit chip in her hand. "Keep that secure. If you lose it, you'll be out here for a lot longer than a couple of years."

"I will. Thank you for your help."

He nodded and left. Sharon gathered up their two bags. Martin realized everyone was loading up their belongings and forming a line at the door.

They'd arrived. His heart beat faster. He was here, at the fringe. He'd made it.

Though he wanted to run to the outer door, to leap down the ramp, it was all he could do to drag himself along behind the others. Excited chatter filled the air, but Martin could barely breathe.

Sharon followed the others out the door and down the ramp, his belongings and hers hanging over one shoulder and one hand clamped down over the pocket that surely held her precious credit chip.

He had to warn her that she was sending a clear signal to thieves. He'd seen it too many times even in the small port of their own plex.

If he didn't warn her, she could lose everything.

"Sharon," he tried to say, but it came out as more of a croak. His knees buckled on the ramp, sending him tumbling down. He landed in a twisted heap of dead-weight limbs on the grimy port floor. His heart beat heavily in his chest, each thump a ponderous hollow thud.

He lost sight of her in the crowd. Sharon was gone.

Bustling activity surrounded him. Men and women in a rainbow of uniforms, many armed, some scarred and others missing limbs, some human, most not, they all went about their business. A jumble of languages reached his ears. So much noise, movers beeping, the deep rumble of ships launching that shook the ground where he lay. The colors and lights overwhelmed him. There was no order here, no evidence of shiny cleaning bots that kept an eye on everyone, no calming ambient music. No one here followed the acceptable public volume level. It was all so raw.

"Ah there you are," said a familiar voice. Arneco came closer and stopped on Martin's hand. "Captain said he'd send movers over to retrieve the stock. And thanks for loaning Carl out. Miracle worker, that one. Got the ship back in phase just before we docked."

"Find your missing person?" asked the

man stationed at the end of the ramp.

"Sadly no. Nothing living can survive the re-alignment. Didn't even find his body. The passengers already depart?"

"Just missed them."

Arneco shrugged. "Just as well. Wasn't looking forward to seeing the widow off after the message your doc sent. Maybe that quick death Martin got was a merciful thing. Dreamer's soul, he was."

"Mercy indeed. Fringe eats dreamers alive." The crewman jutted his chin toward the crowd and shook his head. "Should have seen her. Doubt the widow will last a week."

Their words slurred together until they were no longer discernable from the din that slowly dissolved into a distant hum. Martin tried to grab Arneco's boot, but he couldn't move even a finger. Couldn't blink. He lost track of time between thick, heavy heartbeats.

Martin beheld the wonders of the fringe, the border between the known and unknown. At last, he was free.

SIPPER

Tia Margolis stepped out of the lander and onto a patch of flat orange rock. Sunlight glinted off the city of frosted crystal spires half a kilo away. She held up her hand to block the glare and shifted the bag containing everything she owned to her other shoulder.

Behind her, excited murmurs passed through the single-file line of people flowing from the door. The hungry looks in their eyes, scars, wiry frames, and patched clothes marked them all as the dregs of their homeworld. They'd shared a single meal together after coming out of deep-sleep, a hundred wary roaches guarding their plates while sizing up the competition.

She'd chosen an ally after what she'd seen in that dining hall. One around the same age, a similar weight and build, someone she could hold her own against if it came to that.

"You ready?" she asked Michael.

He gazed at the city ahead of them. "Still excited now that you've seen it?"

She nodded. "A free ride across the system to live in a crystal tower and a job that pays a small fortune? What more can a girl ask for?"

"Oh, I don't know. A nice guy, a place to settle down..."

Tia smacked him on the shoulder and shook her head, laughing. "One ride to the surface side by side doesn't mean we're together. Not like that, anyway."

Avanard Talcott, the crat who'd drawn the short straw to take the trip down to the surface with them, remained on the loading ramp with the same sour look he'd worn since they'd all boarded the lander together. "Three months, roaches. We want to know everything about this city. No reports, no pay."

He too gazed at the sparkling spires, but with a more calculating eye, like he was picking out his future apartment. Likely on the top floor so he could look down on everyone else just like in the towering plexes where the crats lived back home. He probably couldn't wait to get back into deep-sleep so he could preserve his precious flawless complexion while she and the others did all the exploratory dirty work.

It was still better than any work she could have gotten back home, and given the bright sunlight and lack of mud, far less dirty. And the payout, well, she was already considering how to spend more credits than any roach could ever hope to earn.

"Stick close to the city. We're not paying you to wander. Bonuses for those who produce concrete information on the previous occupants or reason for their departure. Now scatter." Avanard's lips twisted with blatant disdain as he waved them away. A second later, he ducked back inside the lander.

She could do without seeing that expression, the one given by every crat she'd ever encountered, for three full months. Tia took a deep breath of the warm clean air while she waited for the last of her fellow explorers to exit so the lander crew could unload the supplies.

She still couldn't believe that the crats were actually feeding her. First time for everything.

Once the last person was down the ramp, a mover unit squeaked its way down onto the ground with a pallet full of crates. It set them down just before the high-stacked load tipped over. Meanwhile, the crew took no care in hurling bins and barrels onto the flat rock. Tia and the others stood back to avoid getting hit.

The moment the mover made it back up the ramp, the lander's doors closed and the engines lit.

Orange sand pelted Tia's body as the ship lifted off. She used the edge of her worn coat to shield her face while her mind was busy going over the supplies she'd seen.

The crats had done a fine job of making sure the supplies were plunder proof: unlabeled, heavily wrapped, and compressed. It would make their work a thousand times harder to open anything out here, releasing all the contents to the wind and sand and expanding them to full size and weight. If there were any advantages, weapons or otherwise, hidden in the stores, she'd have to wait to find it until they got everything into one of the towers and unpacked.

Once the wind settled down enough that she could see again, she darted forward and grabbed an end of one of the larger crates. Michael followed her lead and took the other. They started toward the spires jutting from the expanse of sand. Behind them, the others chose their loads.

Tia walked faster, not willing to let anyone else be the first one to reach the city. She'd been the first one on the lander and the first one off of it. After two months sleeping on the deep space freighter, she needed space to move around.

Open air. Hell, *fresh* air. She breathed deep and laughed at the stupid crats who had recruited her with the offer to leave the over-crowded port city and travel to the great unknown. She'd never dreamed of leaving her homeworld, couldn't have hoped to ever afford it.

This opportunity had only been a distant dream until she'd seen the ad. And then she'd qualified. She still couldn't believe her luck. The crats might be well-fed and healthy under their expensive clothes as they spent their days sitting on comfortable furniture in their spacious, climate-controlled offices, but she, a lowly roach, was here in paradise.

Faceted with randomly distanced bands, the towers glittered like jewels, their tips pointed like giant crystals. Hundreds of them, all clustered together in this one spot on the planet.

Sand and wind ruled the surrounding two-thirds of the planet. On the far side lay an ocean of poisonous water, ringed by a forest of thick tree-like plants. Data from the preliminary scans had favored life in the deserted sparkling city, far from the noxious pollen emitted by the forest.

The sun warmed her skin. Her step was lighter than it had ever been, eating up the yards between her and her temporary new home.

Wind buffeted them, tangling her hair as they walked.

Michael shifted his hold to one hand and wiped his patched sleeve across his glistening brow. "In a hurry?"

"You're not?"

He shrugged. "We've got three months. Let's enjoy them before they ship us back. I don't know about you, but I'm really not looking forward to a couple million bodies crowded around me again."

Her steps slowed. "True."

They reached the open arch of the first spire. She turned to see the others spread out in the sand behind them, a line stretching thinner and thinner between her and where the lander had been.

Michael stopped, staring upward at the spire towering over them. "Do we just go inside?"

"Our instructions were to explore."

"Should we wait for someone?"

Tia laughed. "You scared? We're free people here. No crats or enforcers. Like the guy on the lander said, 'They're sending in the cockroaches.'"

"Actually, he said the crats were going to regret polluting this planet with cockroaches."

"Whatever. They're gone, all the sneering bastards."

She ducked inside, out of the swirling orange sand-filled wind to find a spiraling ramp in the middle of the tower. They set the crate on the open ground floor. Rooms led off from a central ramp that spiraled upward. It was as if the entire structure had been carved from a giant rod of crystal.

Their footsteps sounded hollow as they traveled upward. Hushed whispers drifted up the ramp, announcing the arrival of the other colonists.

"Might as well set up here," Tia called down to the others.

She went as high as the third band before stepping off the ramp and onto a narrow landing. "This is where we part."

"For now." Michael grinned and then continued upward.

She walked around the interior hall that hugged the central shaft. All the rooms opened to the ramp. No doors. What kind of people didn't appreciate privacy?

Tia glanced into the rooms along the level to find they were all identical. She picked one that faced opposite the landing site and went inside. Everything in the tower was made of the same material, as if it had all been carved or melted by means that left the edges smooth. She ran her hands over the cool surface, marveling at the lack of heavy layers of dust. For being long deserted, it was still cleaner than most of the places she'd bedded down in over the years. The facets of the band on the outside ran along the exterior wall of the room, creating a lovely headboard for a raised platform she decided would be her bed.

Despite there being a hundred other people inside the tower and no doors anywhere, the room was silent. How long had it been since she'd heard no one yelling or street noise or countless hushed conversations from others in the shelter? No hum of engines or generators. No sirens or gunfire.

As she spread out her belongings on the bed, Tia hummed bits of a cheery tune she'd heard someone singing on the freighter after she'd awoken from deep-sleep. Music hadn't been something she'd appreciated before. It had always seemed like one of the frivolous things the rich enjoyed. Roaches were silent, doing their best to go unnoticed by the easily offended crats who owned the enforcers.

There wasn't much in her bag, but it was more than she'd ever owned at one time. She didn't remember much the first few years of her childhood—when her family had rented a small house, before her father had lost his job. Before her parents had pawned most everything they'd owned to stay off the streets but ended up getting sick. Without credits for healthcare, she'd lost her parents and siblings one by one. Alone, she'd become one of the skittering shadows looking for a quick job and a meal. Life as a roach meant being on the move more often than not to avoid the enforcers. She was sick of the perpetual motion, but it beat being placed in one of the work camps that no one returned from.

When she'd received her approval for this job, she'd spent the last credits she'd had and called in every favor owed to get three full changes of clothes, a used coat, and new boots. She'd never owned new boots before. They were far stiffer than she was used to, but with all the sand out there, she was glad she'd made the investment. When her three months were up, she'd have enough credits to buy whatever she wanted, including a permanent place to live. She'd had twenty-three years too many of being at the bottom. This was her chance to rise up.

She peered out one of the facets. Seven other spires jutted from the sand within her direct line of sight. Somewhere down in the sand there had to be a foundation and maybe hints as to who had built these towers and what had happened to them. If she had the time and energy to figure those things out, it would mean more credits. But first, she reminded herself, she needed to get her bearings.

The tower offered plenty of space for everyone to spread out. For the first time in her life, she had a room all to herself. She stood in the middle, eyeing the things on the bed. Her clothes fit neatly into a nook in the wall beside the bed. The tarnished button from her father's utilities maintenance uniform and her mother's wire bracelet decorated a shelf-like ridge on the wall. She frowned at the bare sockets on the bracelet that had once housed red stones. Someday soon she'd have enough credits to replace them and never again have to choose between pawning her precious treasures or starving. Of her siblings, she had nothing but fading memories. She wished they could all see her here now, to be with her in this magical, clean, peaceful place.

With a sigh, Tia pondered the lack of a door. This room now held everything she owned, irreplaceable things. Back home, she'd never considered leaving them out in the open. But no one here had doors. They were going to have to trust one another, at least somewhat. With one last look, she shook off her apprehension and returned to the main level.

The others had piled their loads near the crate she and Michael had carried. The jumbled mess would need to be sorted out, but from a quick inventory of what she'd seen come off the lander, there were still more supplies that needed to be carried in. She headed back out. Michael caught up to her in short order.

"You should see the view from the top," he said as he drew close.

"I will, but we've got to get all this inside so we can get the gardens set up, find food for tonight, and locate the blankets. I don't know about the room you picked, but what I'm using for a bed isn't exactly comfy by itself."

"I could keep you warm." He winked.

She groaned. "Keep dreaming. Or better yet, don't."

He chuckled and dropped behind her for a few steps but then caught back up. "How long do you think everyone will stick together?"

"Long enough to divide up what the crats gave us and not a moment longer." She shrugged. "I'm staying. You?"

His brown eyes crinkled as he smiled. "Yeah."

Once they made it back out to the picked-over pile, they surveyed their options. It was all the heavy stuff, the kind that required people to work together. They'd done it once already and she'd suffered only a little flirting for their effort. She was glad to see that he didn't seem to be the sort that took his advances or her declining them too seriously.

"Another crate?" Michael suggested.

"Might as well. Maybe some of the others will follow our example this time."

"Wishful thinking." He grunted as they lifted the crate and started back toward the spire.

Tia made sure to hold her head high and meet the gazes of everyone they passed. She noted that Michael did the same. Roaches didn't show weakness. That got them killed.

Within two hours, everything had been retrieved and then the unpacking and sorting began. Chaos erupted in the base of the spire. Several people filled their bags with various items Tia never caught sight of and left. The majority stuck around. They'd been to enough food lines to know the benefit of waiting for everything to be set up. But few were willing to do the setting up. Tia jumped into the fray and wasn't surprised to see Michael close by, stacking boxes of canned food.

In the faint glow of the lighting tubes they'd set up, Tia surveyed their stores. Garden and water gathering units had been set up along the arching wall. Food, tools, blankets, and transmitters sat in piles. Michael took a quick count of those that had formed a line. The masses took that as their cue to start filing through with their hands and bags ready. Once everyone had received their equal share of supplies, a good half of them wandered out the door. The rest filtered upward, lugging their individual hoards with them.

Michael offered Tia half of one of his cans of beans. They split it in silence, each taking only sips from one of their allotment of water bottles. It would take a day or two for the water units to get up to full working capacity so they could all refill their bottles.

Tia watched the blinking lights on the locator monitor that leaned against the stairwell wall. The green blips blinked every few seconds, updating the locations of a hundred people. Many of them were clumped together in the tower where she stood. The rest were scattered in nearby spires. She guessed they would be even more widespread in a day or two.

Staying with the majority reminded her of the camaraderie of the shelters; they were alone and strangers, but comforted by their similar predicament. She did plan to venture out to explore, but there was safety in numbers, and until she got more comfortable here on this new world, safety outweighed bonus credits.

Exhausted, she parted ways with Michael and carried her heavy armload of supplies up to her room. A quick check of her belongings assured her that nothing had been stolen. Fully clothed and with the pronged multi-tensil she'd used to eat her dinner in hand, she climbed into her bed and fell into a restless sleep.

When the time came the next morning to meet back at the ground level, she found a few of the others already at work. The gardens needed tending, sand needed to be swept out, and there were a lot of spires to explore. She glanced at the locator to get an idea of where everyone else was. The stats numbers in the corner blinked ninety-eight.

Tia bit her lip and glanced from side to side. She approached two women who were tending the garden units.

"Does anyone know what happened to the two missing people?"

One shrugged and went back to work. The other said, "Probably got into a fight. Mind your own business and stay out of trouble."

Tia nodded. Roach's motto right there, she thought to herself. Whatever had befallen the unfortunate, she didn't plan on it happening to her.

With two meals and plenty of water packed in her bag, she grabbed a shovel from the pile by the door and headed out to a distant spire. A warm breeze urged a couple of clouds across the sky, offering an occasional respite from the morning sun. Once she'd passed the seven closest spires, no footprints marred the sand.

The sun was high overhead before she reached her intended destination. In all that time, she'd only spotted two others in the distance. Out here, with the wind in a momentary lull, the silence was even thicker. It was like the entire planet had been sanitized before their arrival.

This spire bore similar bands to the one they'd designated as their base. It listed to the left, as some of them did a few degrees one direction or another. Very few were perfectly straight. Likely from settling into the shifting sands.

How far did they go down? She examined the faceted band that lay against the ground. On her hands and knees, she used the shovel to dig until more sand was caving in than she was scooping out, but found no sign of a foundation. The crystalline tower was the same above and below the surface. She scanned the horizon but didn't spot any mounds where sand might cover a fallen spire. If they were all still standing, she supposed she didn't have to worry about them falling over now.

Tia went inside. She spent the entire day going from room to room, floor to floor until she reached the top. Every room and floor was the same. Not a single item had been left behind by the original occupants. No sand had blown in beyond a trivial amount near the base level archway.

Disappointed with the lack of treasures or advantages of any kind, she made the trek back to the base spire. When she woke the next morning, she grabbed more food and water and set out again, traveling to a more distant tower. For days, she explored, never finding any deviation in the spires other than some had sand drifting inside and some didn't. What kind of people left absolutely nothing behind?

Michael seemed to be minding his own business, but still cast a friendly smile her way when they passed one another in the mornings as they headed out. Some of the spire occupants had designated themselves as roamers, and like what she and Michael were doing, wandered out to other spires to explore. Others focused on digging and sifting through the sand around the base spire and two of the closest to it. As she approached one of the diggers, he stood up and shouted to the others.

"I've found something. A shoe." He waved the torn remains of a brown shoe over his head.

Tia, Michael, and everyone else in earshot ran over to him.

"Looks like it belonged to one of us," the

digger said.

They passed the mangled shoe around, and when it landed in Tia's hands, she was sure of it. The shoe had been through hell. The upper parts were shredded, but the sole bore the manufacturer markings of home.

"It must have belonged to one of the two people who went missing the first night. How far down was it?" Tia passed the shoe to the next pair of hands.

"A meter. I noticed a mound here this morning that wasn't here yesterday. At first, I thought the wind might have blown it here overnight, but then I started finding scraps of metal and cloth. Then the shoe." The digger knelt by the hole and fished out a handful of crushed metal.

Cans of food. Crushed and mangled, empty now, but there was no mistaking the remnants of the labels.

Tia shivered. Whomever or whatever had attacked their people had buried them after ripping their bodies and their supplies to shreds.

"No bodies?" Michael asked.

The digger shook his head. "Not even a fragment of bone, at least not that I've found so far."

"Do we know where they were staying the first night?" asked a woman carrying an empty sifter.

"Over there, I think. That one's clean inside." He looked at the metal in his hands. "I didn't even know their names."

That wasn't a surprise. Other than Michael, she hadn't made any effort to learn the names of the others either. Habit. The not knowing made it easier when they vanished or were dragged off by the enforcers.

Murmurs rolled through the crowd that had gathered. Tia distanced herself from the hole.

"Want to check out the tower?" asked Michael.

"Sure."

Feeling safer with the two of them together, Tia walked with Michael to the spire the digger had indicated. She came to a halt at the entrance, causing him to run into her back.

"What is it?" he asked, peering over her shoulder.

"He said it was clean, but look." She stepped aside so he could take in the complete lack of sand.

Not a single footprint marred the pristine floor, like someone had come through with a giant vacuum and done a thorough cleaning. Even the sand where they stood in the doorway sloped downward as though it had fallen in but had been removed.

"No way two people did all this," Michael said. "In the towers I've investigated, including the base we first entered, all had at least some sand inside, and you can't help but track it in with you."

Tia nodded. "No one left with anything beyond a shovel, blankets, and food. They couldn't have done this."

Michael raised an eyebrow. "The city is haunted by a fastidious cleaning crew?"

"That crushes and shreds garbage." Tia stepped back, needing to be in the sunlight again.

"We're not garbage," he said softly. "We'll figure this out." He turned back toward the base spire. "Come on."

Glad to see she wasn't the only one who wanted to be away from the sterile tower, Tia let him lead. She didn't even quite mind sitting beside him at the evening meal while the digger told the others what he'd found and she added what little they'd discovered. A couple of roamers said that they'd also come across a sand-free tower further out, but beyond that, there was only speculation.

Tia spent a good deal of the night wondering why the death of two strangers here bothered her more than it would have back home. People vanished all the time. Their clothes turned up on the backs of others who might have been the ones to do the deed or who just happened to be in the right place to grab supplies the dead no longer needed. Both could be true or claimed, and the safest policy was always to keep her suspicions to herself.

The crats wouldn't have placed a killer in with their exploratory crew. As much as they might want the roaches exterminated back home, it was the very fact they could survive that made them useful here. The crats wanted answers about this city, and they wouldn't get them if their explorers were all dead.

Unless...one of her fellow roaches had decided to sweeten the payout pot by lessening their numbers.

Tia pondered the shoe she'd held in her hand. They'd all been thoroughly searched for weapons before boarding the freighter and before entering the lander. None of them possessed anything that would have shredded a person like the damage to the shoe suggested. With her tired mind at a loss for answers, Tia went to her room and gave in to sleep.

Weeks passed without further incident, serving as a balm for the initial unease over the loss of two of their number. As they did back home, they went about their business here. They focused on finding the answers the crats sought and earning the payout that would change their lives forever.

Well over half of the roaches had spread from the base tower to others, expanding the circle of exploration. Tia had marked a month on her wall before her morning tracker board check revealed six more people had gone missing overnight.

As spread thin as they were throughout the city, it took a day to track down the tower where the six had been living. Like the other, it was devoid of sand or sign of life. They set up a watch of diggers and sifters around the perimeter of the tower, and within three days, were rewarded with the discovery of a mound. The diggers hesitantly went to work, uncovering what was left deep within the sand. Sifters worked their baskets to find the shredded remnants of supplies and clothing that were all that remained of the missing six.

Tia shared one of her cans with Michael in the shade of the nearest spire while the apprehensive crowd dissipated, filtering back to the towers where they'd been working before the disappearance.

"No one saw anyone bury them here," Michael said.

"It sort of bubbled up from below, like a

mound in the sand that wasn't there the day before. That's what I heard."

They took turns passing the can back and forth until the cubed meat and beans were gone. Tia licked her multi-tensil clean and shoved it back in the pocket on the leg of her pants.

"No one heard anything that night?" he asked.

Tia shook her head. "Not that I know of. As much as I'd like a bonus, I'll settle for making it to payout. I'm staying inside."

"For two months?" Michael laughed. "You? You wouldn't last three days inside.

She grinned. "You have a point. Watch each other's backs?"

He used a finger to clean out the last remnants of food and then slid the empty can into the bag slung over his shoulder and stood, offering her a hand up. "Thought we already were."

She hadn't been so sure lately but was relieved that they had an official understanding. She didn't trust anyone lightly, but Michael, for all his lighthearted flirting, did seem sincere. And if something out there was able to take six people down at a time, she had to admit that it was more than she could handle alone.

When the remaining twenty-two that were still living at the base tower returned that night, Tia suggested they set up sentry duty. No one argued. Volunteers created a schedule in a matter of minutes.

Thirteen more explorers living elsewhere in the city went missing that night. Runners went out from the base spire to inform the others and to learn if anyone had seen or heard anything. No one had.

Fear brought everyone back together for a meeting in the base spire. Accusations flew of a killer among them. Others were sure there was a hungry creature on the loose. Tia sat beside Michael, staring dismally at the seventy-nine remaining dots all congregated in one place.

Beside her, the water units dripped, filtering moisture from the air and the breaths of so many people gathered together inside the spire. People covered the floor much as they had that first day when they had arrived. But so many were missing now. Looking at those who remained, she couldn't conjure up even one of them. Nameless blank faces. Was that what it was like for the crats?

She wasn't one of them. These were people. Her people.

While the others wove their accusations and conspiracies into elaborate tales, she took note of the people bathed in the grow lights, cataloging them in her mind with as much care as the inventory of food supplies hidden in her room. The people ranged from her age to salt-and-pepper-haired and spanned a wide palette of skin colors. All appeared in relative good health as that had been one of the qualifications. The one thing they all seemed to share at the moment was a shadow of fear on the faces she now resolved to put names to.

A curfew was suggested and agreed upon. No one would be outside the spires after dark. No one would go off alone during the day. They would all watch out for each other. Tia was convinced that it was more to see who knew what was going on, or who was causing this than to protect one another. But either way, she wasn't going to argue.

When she went up to her room that night, she discovered Michael had moved from the top of the tower to the room next to hers. He caught her staring as she paused outside his room on the way to her own.

"You don't mind, do you? Hard to do that back-watching thing with several floors between us," he said.

Tia shook her head. She leaned against his doorway. "What will you do after payout?"

"Find my brothers and get us a place to live. You?"

"I'm hoping we can figure out what's

happening here. I have nothing to go back to. I'd like to stay."

"I'm sure the crats will take care of whatever it is. They don't trust us with weapons, but you can bet they'll send a squad of enforcers in to clean out whatever is doing this."

She nodded.

Michael motioned for her to come in. Tia sat on a squared-off protrusion from the floor.

"You'd want to stay once the crats take over?" he asked.

"Can't be worse than where we came from. Besides, it would take a while for it to get as crowded as it is back home. I can breathe here."

"I know what you mean." He smiled sadly. "If it weren't for the fact that transport fees for my brothers would eat up all my payout, I'd probably stay too."

She stayed talking to Michael for longer than she'd planned, trying to envision what this world would look like under crat rule. When she finally crawled into bed, her mind kept going back to the mess the crats would make. Sure, they'd bring weapons to track down whatever was picking people off, but they'd also bring laws and restrictions and enforcers. They'd set up labor camps. They wouldn't want roaches in their new pristine city or to mar the landscape with affordable housing. They'd skew the economy in their favor, forcing any remaining roaches to quickly fall back into squalor. She'd find herself in a labor camp, far from the sight of this city, sewing fashionable clothes or whatever else the crats desired, in order to earn her next meal.

Disheartened by the thought of these beautiful spires crawling with pompous crats, throwing around their credits and kicking her kind out into the sands to die, Tia stared into the darkness.

Maybe she could convince the landing team that this was a terrible place and they'd leave the remaining roaches behind out of spite. Surely, if her fellow explorers worked together, they could catch whatever was attacking them. With the garden and water units established, they had plenty to eat and drink. There were enough tools and replacement parts to work from if anything went wrong. She'd done without comforts all her life. Living out from under the crat rule was payment enough. While contemplating what to put into her report, Tia drifted off to sleep.

Seven more lights had gone dark by morning.

Michael stood beside her, staring at the locator as if he expected more lights to wink out any second. She placed one of the hard protein-fortified biscuits from her stash into his hand.

"It's bad enough people are getting killed, but does whatever this is have to destroy the supplies too?" she asked.

"I'm guessing there will be another mound in a couple of days. Another garden and water unit gone." Michael glanced around the room. "We're not letting anyone else leave with one. They can come back here to restock if they want to move out. Though I don't know why they would want to leave. Seems safest here."

"You're prepared to enforce that decree?" she asked.

"Are you prepared to help me enforce it?"

Tia considered what she wanted to eat for the remainder of her stay. It wasn't what was in the cans. "Yes, I suppose I am."

When Michael explained his reasoning to the others living in their spire that evening, no one disagreed. It may have helped that they were able to share the first batch of tomatoes while the matter was being discussed, but Tia let Michael believe it was his compelling argument that swayed the group.

The occupants of the base spire spent their days roaming nearby. Some continued to dig, others sought out spires they could reach in half a day's journey and returned by nightfall. All of them traveled with a partner and while there were no great discoveries, they remained alive.

The board informed them daily that those who were scattered elsewhere were not so fortunate.

As their population dwindled further, speculation spread through those that remained at the base tower, wondering if the city was haunted, perhaps cursed. Tia had never believed in such nonsense. Yet, she couldn't dispute that something was out there hunting people down at night and no one had yet to find any clues as to who or what it was.

"Do you think we should check in with anyone staying nearby to see if they've seen anything we haven't?" Michael asked.

"Not a bad idea. I'll go with you."

They gathered up a day's worth of supplies, consulted the locator for the last known whereabouts of those who had most recently gone missing, and informed the sentries of their plans. Feeling secure in their preparations, they set out into the sun and sand. Wind buffeted them as they walked but it brought no relief from the heat.

A quick search of the first tower revealed it was as clean and empty as the others they'd searched before. The second was the same. No sign of footprints remained outside the spires other than their own. It was like the other explorers had never existed.

"Guess we better be sure to keep shoveling out the sand," said Tia. "Whatever is doing this likes things tidy."

Michael chuckled, the sound echoing through the main level of the tower. "Who knew cleanliness kept the monsters away?"

A hollow ominous silence filled the tower after the echo subsided. It was all too still, too quiet, too clean.

"We should go," Tia said.

"You feel it too?"

She nodded toward the door, unwilling to speak another word aloud.

Outside, the wind had picked up, blowing sand at their faces. Tia pulled her shirt up to cover her nose and mouth. Squinting against the pelting grains, she and Michael hurried toward the nearest occupied spire. No sentries were on duty, but the digger who'd found the first shoe in the sand met them with a scowl as they ducked inside.

"What are you doing here? I hope you don't plan on moving in, not unless you brought supplies and a lot of them."

"We came to check on you," said Tia.

"Get out and mind your own damn business."

"Have you had contact with any of the others?" Michael asked.

His eyes narrowed. "I suppose you're gonna tell me that you're the last ones left and you need a place to stay."

Michael rested his hand on Tia's shoulder. "Not at all. Just making sure you're all right. More have disappeared but many of us are safe at the base spire. You're always welcome to come back."

"Disappeared." He scoffed. "Shredded. That's what they were. Nothing else explains what I dug up. Shredded and eaten, the rest spit out."

In light of the gruesome images flashing through her head, Tia relished the warmth of Michael's hand and the fact that he was mere inches away. "We'll leave you to it then."

"You do that. Go lure whatever that thing is somewhere else. I got a family to feed back home. I need that payout, and if there are fewer bodies to share it with, I'm not complaining."

They made a hasty exit before he got it in his mind to reduce the population by two more.

"Let's check all the towers as we go," Tia suggested.

They ducked into each one along the way. Some had drifts of sand up to her knees, others only a fine dusting. They even ran across footprints of roamers in some of them. But for all they welcomed the signs of life, they found no clues as to what had happened to the others.

When they returned to the base, Tia went back to the locator. "I'm going to stay up and watch it. People have to be going somewhere when they vanish."

"I'll get some sleep," Michael said. "I'll take over in a few hours."

Tia nodded, already staring at the forty-eight remaining green lights. His footsteps retreated up the ramp and away. The chatting of the sentries turned to white noise as she focused on keeping all the lights in view at once. Slowly, she counted from one to forty-eight over and over, verifying that everyone was there.

A woman she'd come to know as Ellen handed her two crisp leaves of deep green lettuce, each bigger than her hand. She savored each crunchy bite, her taste buds tingling with joy as she kept her count timed with her chewing. For a few moments, the terrors haunting them seemed far away.

Tia spared a moment of her watch to glance around the room, repeating the names she'd learned of the people she'd been living alongside in the base spire. Other than her family, they'd been with her longer than most others throughout her life. She'd come to trust the current pair of sentries, Clive and Jamal. They were large men who, had she encountered them alone back home, would have sent her scurrying in the opposite direction, but here their physical strength offered peace of mind.

True to his word, Michael replaced her halfway through the night. She went up the ramp with the sleepy-eyed sentries whose shift had also ended. Asleep within minutes of stretching out on her bed, she dreamed of the angry digger and forty-eight green lights blinking in the darkness.

When she woke, she went down to relieve Michael. All the lights remained, now moving over the board as people went about their day.

"Get some sleep," she told him. "They don't vanish in the day. Are you up for watching again tonight?"

He yawned, then nodded and headed back up the ramp.

Tia went outside with a few of the others who were gatherers, learning how they used the test kits the crats provided to take samples from the ground at different depths and of the spire walls and the air. All of these things were then brought back inside and scanned or entered and then transmitted back to the pampered and wealthy who were safe far away.

She wondered what the spire would sound like filled with the shrill forced laughter and perpetual gossip of the crats. Their music thumping against the crystalline walls. All their gadgets transmitting signals. The shadows of a gridwork of personal transports would block the sun overhead as they wove their way between the spires.

The only way she could prevent them from ruining this place was to convince the crats they didn't want to come here. She passed the rest of her day entering the beginnings of her report on the palm-sized transmitter, detailing the losses of the roaches, the heartiest of humanity. She talked about the endless heat, the pelting winds, and the war they fought with the blowing sand that snuck inside no matter how well they shook out their clothes or emptied out their shoes.

Michael came down, suggesting that she take a nap and that he would take the early evening shift at the board. She explained her plan with her report and he grinned.

"I'll tell the others. If we all go along with it, there's a hope we can convince the crats they don't want to settle here."

"They can come kill whatever it is that's out there or maybe toss us a few weapons so we can do it ourselves, but we don't need them here. We've sacrificed more than enough of us to have a claim to this place." Tia grabbed a ripe, juicy tomato from a nearby unit, and took a bite as she headed for the ramp. Michael was already busy telling Edward and Sylvia, a pair of roamers, about her idea. Their laughter followed her up to her room.

It was completely dark when she came down to find Michael's glum face staring at the board.

"What is it?" she asked as she began the count of lights and within that first glance, realized how many were missing. "Twenty-six people gone? What happened? Where did they go?"

He turned to her. Clive and Jamal, watched them both intently from the doorway.

"They just blinked out. One second they were there, then they blinked out one by one." He clutched his hands together. "They were there, in three different towers, and then they weren't. I saw one go, then another and another." His voice shook. "We're the only occupied tower left."

Tia sunk to the floor in front of the board. "How can that be? They can't just vanish."

Jamal gave up pretending to care about what was outside and came over to the board, staring and counting the remaining lights. Tia joined him, trying to wrap her mind around what Michael had said.

"Only twenty-two of us left?" Jamal looked at her as though he'd hoped he'd miscounted.

He hadn't. She nodded.

"You think the crats are behind this?" she asked. "They don't have to pay us if we're not here in three weeks. Do they have a way of siphoning us off the planet? Sucking up a few at a time and shoving us back into those deep-sleep pods? They'll probably try to convince us we never left, that this place was all a dream."

Clive deserted his post to join them. He stood with his arms crossed over his broad chest. His hopeful tone belied his stance. "You think they're all alive somewhere, not torn to bits and eaten by something?"

"I wouldn't put it past the crats," said Michael. "They have all the data we've been gathering and the reports that have been transmitted so far. We should have withheld everything until payoff."

Dread settled into Tia's stomach, weighing her down and sucking her ambition dry. The report she'd entered was based on the others disappearing. If the crats were behind it, her warnings were meaningless. They were probably laughing at every word.

"If this is the crats, how do you think they're finding us?" asked Jamal.

"They have access to the locator board, which tracks our transmitters. They have to know if there's anyone left to pick up and where they are," Tia said.

"Then we destroy it and the transmitters," Michael said.

Tia glanced at the board they'd been watching so diligently. "If we do destroy the board, the crats might not come back for us at all."

Clive's hands formed fists and his face took on a dark glower. "You can't do that! I have a family to go home to. They're depending on my payout."

Michael, though shorter and much thinner, stared him down. "So do I. But they'll survive. That's what we roaches do, isn't it?"

"But if they're somehow getting us off this world in small batches, they're not killing us. We want to be found. I want to get back home," said Jamal.

Tia shook her head. "If they're being all sneaky about taking us offworld, do you think they're really going to let us go home? More likely, they'll drop us in some labor camp to avoid paying us."

Ellen, who had come to stand beside Tia, stepped forward. "That sounds exactly like something the crats and their damned enforcers would do. Keeping their hands clean by not outright killing us is what they do best, isn't it?"

Jamal's fists clenched at his sides and his

voice rose. "I suppose you're going to tell me the buried, shredded supplies are a ploy to set us against one another? They think we'll wipe ourselves out?"

Clive took a few steps toward Tia and Michael, his face the dark and threatening one Tia had imagined would send her running back home. It would have here too, except she had Ellen and Michael beside her.

"I'm not willing to take that chance. No one better do anything stupid or they'll answer to me," said Clive.

Ellen surged forward to get in his face. "If these two are right, destroying that board might be the only way of making sure we live until the end of our assignment. If the crats can't find us from above, they'll have to come down to the surface. And if they're down here, they're on our territory now."

Clive shoved her backward. "What are we going to do? Attack them with shovels? They have guns, woman. Use your head."

In a blur of motion, Michael grabbed one of the shovels leaning against the wall and swung it at the locator board. Another hard swing tore through the electronics and hit the crystalline wall with a reverberating clang. Jamal and Clive rushed him. Jamal ripped the shovel from Michael's hands while Clive took a swing at his head.

"Stop," yelled Tia.

They didn't listen. The three men fought until Michael sank to the ground clutching his ribs with one hand and wiping blood from his nose with the other.

"You had no right," yelled Clive.

Jamal threw his transmitter at Tia's feet. "Just in case you're right. But you and your friend there better pray that the crats *do* come for us. If they don't, you won't have to worry about settling in."

The two men stormed up the ramp to their rooms. Tia glanced around to find their raised voices and the destruction of the board had brought the rest of the spire's occupants rushing down to the main floor. The scowls and glares surrounding her made her shrink. Only Ellen stood beside her and Michael. A low muttering filled the air, punctuated by loud swearing and several threats. Tia jumped when the first transmitter hit the ground by her feet. Another followed. Several hit her and Michael. They littered the floor in short order.

The crowd dispersed upward. Ellen helped Tia destroy the transmitters with a couple of shovels outside. Michael leaned against the arched doorway watching them as the blowing sand accepted their offering.

"I'll take a sentry shift," Ellen said. "Give them all a bit to cool down. You did the right thing."

Tia smiled at the kind-faced middle-aged woman and took the shovels back inside. She helped Michael up the ramp.

"Maybe you should stay in my room tonight," she offered. "They're pretty angry. I wouldn't put it past them to come after you again."

His face was red and already starting to swell. "Thanks. I'll get my things. Might find them out in the sand in the morning otherwise."

Tia nodded. Her bed wasn't big enough for two, but he'd be safe enough on the floor. It wasn't like the bed was any more comfortable. All the surfaces were the same hard crystal.

Michael returned with his things and settled on the floor with his blanket, using his extra clothes as a pillow.

Listening for any footsteps outside her room, Tia eventually fell into a restless sleep.

By morning, the rift between the spire's occupants and the two of them was clear enough. She and Michael stayed together for the next week, tending the gardens, maintaining the filters on the water units, and shoveling the ever creeping sand from the floor of the main level. They left the exploring to the others, sticking close to their belongings and their food supplies for fear of retribution.

A howling wind woke Tia in the middle of the night. She sat up and peered out the facet by her bed to see nothing out of the ordinary in the moonlight. She had just decided to crawl back under her blanket when a faint shudder traveled through the tower. Then came another. This one was stronger, moving through her bed and the walls around her, knocking her family treasures from their shelf.

Michael jumped to his feet. "What is that?"

"I don't know."

She'd had plenty of practice with raids at all hours, and though she wasn't sure if this was the crats coming for them, habit took over. She grabbed her pack and shoved clothes, the cans of food she'd hidden around her room, and her family treasures into it. Satisfied that she had everything, she slung it over her back and bolted out the door. Michael was right beside her with his own bulging bag as she raced down the ramp. Another tremor shook the spire. She could hear others calling out, panicked as the two of them fled downward.

"Where should we go? You think it's the crats?" Michael asked.

Her heart raced. "This was our last known location. If they're coming, they'll look here first.

We should go."

"Grab a garden. I'll get a water unit. If we're moving out, we're taking them with us."

The howling took on an odd pitch. Tia realized it wasn't the wind, but something else. Something deeper, hollow-sounding, like a long, anguished gasp. Her gaze darted over the vibrating interior of the spire.

"Get out. Everyone out," she yelled.

Michael hefted a water unit into his arms, shifting the weight until the sloshing was minimized. "What the hell was that?"

The ground on the main level shifted, spiraling slowly outward from the center. Tia darted to the door, hefting a heavy garden as she went. Michael was right behind her, water splashing out of the unit, soaking his sleeves.

The floor dilated to reveal a black pit. The ramp shook, vibrating violently.

Tia gulped. Her ears popped. Someone's shirt, followed by a shoe, tumbled down the ramp. An empty food can clattered by. Above them, someone screamed. The can fell to the main level and down into the pit. The shoe and shirt followed close behind.

She stepped back, making sure her feet were firmly outside the door. They could see the vibrations, feel them in the doorway itself, but the ground outside remained steady. Michael peered over her shoulder, his ragged breath hot in her ear. The remaining garden and water units, shovels, and all but one light plunged into the hole.

The pit opened wider until all that remained was a narrow ledge beside the outer wall. But there was no way to get to it. No way for anyone above to escape. The ramp spiraled down into the depths of the pit. Clothing, trinkets, and cans tumbling down it into the gaping maw.

Sylvia plummeted in a second later. And then Jamal, their screams fading as they fell.

"Help us," cried Ellen, clutching at the ramp and finding no purchase. She disappeared into the hole.

Others joined them, each one fighting to hold on, but the entire tower quivered sharply, emitting a barely audible mind-numbing sound that froze Tia's body in place.

Edward tumbled down the ramp, with Clive right behind him, both with arms and legs flailing as they fought to slow their decent. The relentless suction tugged at Tia's clothing even from where she stood outside the door. The two men knocked into one another, both losing their battle and plummeting into the hole.

All she could do was watch as everyone fell to their death. It had to be death. The screams seemed to fade rather than come to any sudden end.

"We can't help them," Michael said.

"I know." But it didn't make hearing them any easier to bear. Tears ran down her cheeks. She repeated their names to herself, names she knew now, names that had faces that she'd never see again. Would anyone else remember them?

This wasn't the crats. And while a small part of her mind was relieved that the distant eyes on her reports weren't mocking her naiveté, the horror of what was before her drowned out any degree of celebration. And now they'd destroyed their transmitters and the board. Would anyone come?

The shaking continued after the last body had fallen into the blackness, and still longer until the last of the belongings had trickled downward and the sole remaining light toppled into the pit. Then finally, it stopped. The floor closed off, again forming a solid surface without any sign of the spiral pattern that had been dilated only moments ago.

Inside, nothing remained to show they had lived there. Pristine as the day they had arrived, the crystalline spire greeted them with its silence.

The sucking gasps of whatever lived deep beneath the sand haunted her. She had to get further away. Too close. They were standing too close.

Michael backed away, nudging her to follow him. They walked to the nearest spire but didn't go inside. Instead, they settled into the cool sand and huddled inside their coats.

They were alone here. Just the two of them. A sob rose in her throat.

Michael wrapped his arms around her. "Two weeks. We can do this."

"We're not going back inside one of those things," she decreed.

"Definitely not."

She sat up, pulling away, and wiped her hands over her face. "What do you think is down there, sipping its meal through these straws?"

"I don't intend to find out."

"Me either." She took a deep shuddering breath and exhaled slowly. As the moon crept its way across the sky, her mind began to work again. "Do you think it's random? Which straws it uses? Or did it sense we were here?"

"My guess is random. Or maybe it has a cycle, like working from the center outward. If it had sensed us, I think all the digging, especially around our spire, would have triggered it earlier."

Tia looked to the flat expanse of rock where the lander would return. "It's not a city at all."

"It would seem not."

"We were living inside a giant feeding tube." She shuddered.

"When you put it that way..." He cringed.

Tia felt his soaked shirt rub against her arm. "How much water do we have?"

Michael opened the unit and felt around inside. "Enough to get by if we stay in the shade.

The sun would be up soon and would be beating down on them unless they stayed in the shadows of the spires.

"We'll have to keep moving," she said. "What about the crats? What do we tell them?"

"If they come for us, you mean?"

Tia nodded.

"About the straws or the fact that there are only two of us left?"

"Both."

He brushed some of the sand from his hair and settled back against the wall of the spire. "The truth, I guess."

"If we live long enough to tell them the truth."

"We will." He took her hand and squeezed it.

"Think they'll pay us when we give them the bad news?"

"I don't much care anymore. I just want off this planet," he said.

"But without credits..." She put her head in

her hands. It was one thing to live in a shelter where she'd been able to afford their minimal charges. But out on the streets, that was just waiting for death, no different from sitting there in the sand.

"They'll pay us. They need our report," he assured her.

As if ninety-eight dead wasn't enough information. She leaned against the wall beside Michael, watching the sky turn pink. Wind blew between the spires. Tia dug through her hastily packed bag, taking stock of their food supply. She slipped her mother's bracelet onto her arm, needing the faint memory of comfort.

They spent the next two weeks rationing the canned food they'd grabbed and slowly decimating everything the garden unit had to offer. They took turns sleeping against one another, sharing warmth during the long nights while keeping watch for any sign of the lander or indication that whatever was below the surface could reach them even outside the feeding tubes.

Though they tried to use their coats to form a small shelter during the day, blowing sand kept them from talking much and wore their exposed skin raw. It also clogged the water filters days before the scheduled pick up. All the tools to fix them had been sucked underground. At a loss, they drank what the garden unit gathered to water it's now depleted crops, but its filters were half-clogged too, leaving what little water it did produce bitter and gritty.

Thirsty, starving, and continually pelted by sand, Tia and Michael greeted the speck in the sky with whoops of joy. The lander settled on the rocky pad. Uniformed crewmembers along with several enforcers spilled from its door.

Michael draped his arm around her shoulders and grinned. "See, I told you we'd make it."

The crew drifted closer, spinning around slowly with hand-held scanners. They used hand signals and remained silent as the group split up. When they reached the spire that had been the base, a couple slid inside, their scanners extended like weapons.

One poked his head through the archway. "Clear."

Three men approached the spire where she and Michael sat. "We've got some live ones," one of them called out.

Others joined them as they gathered around Tia and Michael. Avanard Talcott stepped forward, a scowl on his face. "Where are the rest of the roaches?"

His condescension made her skin crawl but she put on her best defiant stare. "Aren't we supposed to get paid before we file our final reports?"

The enforcers with Talcott laughed. Four of them drew weapons.

Michael held up his hands. "The rest of us are dead."

One of the crewmen held up a scanner and shook it in Michael's face. "I can see that, moron. Where are the bodies?"

Tia stood up slowly, holding onto Michael's shoulder to keep a wave of dizziness from taking her down. "What's the range of those things?"

"Three kilometers."

"They left."

"Left?" Talcott's eyebrows scrunched together. "Where the hell would they go? This is where you were told to stay."

"I know." She sighed. "We tried to tell them that, didn't we, Michael?"

Michael gave her a questioning look. She pinched his shoulder.

"Yeah. Wouldn't listen," he said.

Tia pointed to the empty garden unit. "They left us here, gave us one unit, and took off a couple weeks ago." She shook her head. "Like he said, they're dead now. They have to be. The ocean and forest are too far away and they're poisonous."

The scowl didn't leave Talcott's face. "Then why would they go?"

"How often does a roach get to live in a place like this? Never. And you were going to make them leave." She shrugged. "They were taking their chances."

"Doubt there's anything left to find by now. Saves us some time." He nodded to one of the enforcers who didn't have a weapon in his hands. "Transfer their credits."

The man pulled out a datapad and half-looked at it as he slid his fingers around. Whatever he was doing, his fingers never actually touched the surface and his gaze never left Talcott's.

Emptiness filled her gut, like the floor of the spire, spiraling open, and sucking all hope of a better life into the sand at her feet. She reached into her bag and felt around until her fingers hit the button that had belonged to her father. She clutched it in her hand and tried not to think about the empty wire frame around her wrist that would never hold another stone.

Talcott smoothed down his perfectly tailored lightweight jacket and tugged the sleeves into place before turning back to Tia. "So then, your report?"

"Can we give it to you in the lander? We could use some water, and a meal, and..."

"Start talking, roach."

Tia stared at the weapons. They might as

well have gone down the straw with the rest.

Michael stood up beside her. He clutched her empty hand. His voice was hollow. "The city is perfect."

"Yes," she said. "We had no issues with the garden units. When all of them were functioning properly, before the others left, we had plenty of water and food. The beds are a bit hard, but other than that, no real complaints."

The man with the datapad handed it to Talcott. He glanced at it. "And your reports? The claims you made?"

Tia sighed, dropping her gaze to the sand. "False. We really wanted to stay, well, until the others left us here alone."

"Where are all of your things? We can't have roach trash lying around when the rest of us arrive."

"They took everything when they left," Michael said.

Talcott snickered. "Sounds like you made some good friends."

Friends. She'd never considered calling them that, but perhaps they were. Their faces flashed through her mind, the ones she'd made an effort to get to know, and the ones she'd only noted in passing. For a moment, the memory of their screams drowned out whatever Talcott was saying to his men.

He handed the datapad back to the enforcer and pulled a com cube from his pocket. He held it up, turning slowly until a green light lit. "Clean up will be complete momentarily. We're all clear here. Send the first wave down."

"Down? Now?" asked Michael.

"How many?" Tia asked.

Talcott tapped the cube once. The light went out and he dropped it back into his pocket. "A couple thousand. They've been waiting in deep-sleep since we dropped you off. I can't wait for them to see our new home."

Michael squeezed her hand so hard she bit her lip to keep from yelping. "I hope you all enjoy it here," he said.

Blood rushed in her ears as she stared at the enforcers. A light flashed. A loud pop. The pressure on her hand was gone. Michael toppled over and landed at her feet.

Before she had a chance to cry out, the flash came again. Tia imagined thousands of crats spilling from a fleet of landers. A pop. Lines of them trailed into the spires, filling them. Pain erupted in her chest. Wind whipped at the crats, sending them running for the safety of the spires. She dropped to her knees. The crystal shook. Hot sand licked her cheek as darkness crept into her vision. The floor opened up and devoured them all.

About the Author

Jean Davis lives in West Michigan with her musical husband, two attention-craving terriers and a small flock of chickens and ducks. When not ruining fictional lives from the comfort of her writing chair, she can be found devouring books and sushi, weeding her flower garden, or picking up hundreds of sticks while attempting to avoid the abundant snake population that also shares her yard. She writes an array of speculative fiction.

She is the author of *The Narvan* series and several standalone books including *A Broken Race*, *Sahmara*, *The Last God* and *Destiny Pills and Space Wizards*.

Read her blog, *Discarded Darlings*, and sign up for her mailing list at www.jeandavisauthor.com. You'll also find her on Facebook and Instagram at JeanDavisAuthor, and on Goodreads and Amazon.

Made in the USA
Middletown, DE
06 July 2020

10930373R00099